DESERT DRIVE

This Large Print Book carries the
Seal of Approval of N.A.V.H.

DESERT DRIVE

A WESTERN QUINTET

PETER DAWSON

THORNDIKE PRESS
A part of Gale, Cengage Learning

GALE
CENGAGE Learning®

Detroit • New York • San Francisco • New Haven, Conn • Waterville, Maine • London

LIBRARY OF CONGRESS CATALOGING-IN-PUBLICATION DATA

Dawson, Peter, 1907–1957.
  [Short stories. Selections]
  Desert drive : a western quintet / by Peter Dawson.
    pages ; cm. — (Thorndike Press large print western)
    ISBN 978-1-4104-4843-9 (hardcover) — ISBN 1-4104-4843-6 (hardcover)
  1. Western stories. 2. Large type books. I. Dawson, Peter, 1907–1957.
  Bullets starve a fever. II. Title.
  PS3507.A848A6 2012
  813'.54—dc23   2012007655

Published in 2012 by arrangement with Golden West Literary Agency.

Printed in the United States of America
1 2 3 4 5 6 7 16 15 14 13 12

TABLE OF CONTENTS

BULLETS STARVE A FEVER

This story under this title was submitted by Jon Glidden's agent to Street & Smith's *Western Story Magazine* on January 15, 1938. The story was accepted for publication on March 1, 1938 and appeared in the issue dated May 28, 1938. The author was paid $202.50 upon publication.

I

Ira Peace was eighty-four when he died. If he had known that his death would bring on the Big Bend cattle war, it's barely possible that his iron will would have carried him through a few more years. But even if he had known, it wouldn't have helped, for if Peace had lived to be 120, Major Hewes and Bill Fears would have had it out anyway.

Ira Peace's forty-four sections of range lay between the two bigger outfits, blanketing a rough triangle on the east bank where the southward-flowing Bull River took a wide trend. Peace had been the first man in that country, had taken the pick of the grass. Now that he was dead, it was a toss-up as to who would in the end own his land.

Bill Fears ran his Pitchfork to the north, while Major Hewes's Broad Arrow was down the river. For a year after Peace died, neither man made a bid on those forty-four sections, knowing that the other would make a fight for it. So it hung on that way, Fears quietly hiring a few hardcase riders who drifted into town; the major was satisfied with the fourteen cowpunchers that filled his bunkhouse. Things were lining up for a showdown.

During the second winter both Hewes and Fears claimed a loss of stock far above the winter-kill average. The following summer was a busy one, and still the herds thinned. Major Hewes, a man nearing fifty and used to having his way after a long life spent in the Army from which he had retired not many years before, stormed into town to see the sheriff on three different occasions.

"It's damned easy to work my Broad Arrow brand into a Pitchfork," he announced publicly. "And damned hard to work it the other way around." He didn't come out openly and name Bill Fears as a rustler, but the implication was there. Fears, fifteen years younger, only smiled and said nothing when he heard it.

Tom O'Daniels, for thirty years a lawyer in Bend City, did his best to sell Ira Peace's outfit. But, even at the ridiculously low price O'Daniels was asking, no rancher within 500 miles of Bend City would step into the middle of this smoldering enmity. Peace's relatives were setting up a howl for their money.

Early that next fall, O'Daniels paid a call on Sheriff Wiley. The result was that the sheriff called a meeting of all the ranchers in the county. Asked to state his reasons for the meeting, Wiley wouldn't budge from an evasive answer: "It'll settle a lot o' things. If you're interested, come and sit in."

They did, every last owner in the Big Bend country. Wiley had picked the biggest room in the hotel, and at nine o'clock in the morning, an hour before the time set for the meeting, the room was so over-crowded that the sheriff had to ask all but property owners to leave. The crews, the curious, and the loafers drifted down into the lobby of the River House. One man counted eighteen of Bill Fears's riders grouped on one side of the lobby, all wearing guns in low-slung holsters. Across the room, trying to be casual about it, were eight or nine of

Hewes's Broad Arrow men with only an occasional weapon showing, and this rammed through its wearer's belt. Major Hewes didn't hire gunmen.

At ten, when Sheriff Wiley stepped into the upstairs room, pushed his way through the throng, and banged on the table for silence, his old, lined face wore a troubled look. Wiley was fond of his bottle, and had rested his boots on the bar rail of every saloon in southern Colorado, but the smoke fog now rapidly filling the room was the worst he had ever seen. He blinked his red-rimmed brown eyes and bawled out: "Why in blazes don't someone throw up a window?"

Bill Fears was sitting on the sill of one of the room's two windows. His handsome, dark face broke into a broad smile as he reached around and threw up the sash.

"Better, Sheriff?" he queried, and not a man in the room missed the arrogant edge to his smooth tone. Fears was like that; he didn't have many friends in this crowd, yet he seemed the strongest man there.

Major Hewes, standing along the wall near the door, didn't even look at Fears. But the hostility between these two men made the room vibrant with tension. Each was strong in his own way. Fears was short, stocky, powerful. Hewes stood straight, his gray eyes and white hair, along with his short-clipped and pointed white beard, giving him a distinguished look.

When Wiley finally spoke, many a man breathed a sigh of relief, for the sheriff's words broke a silence that had become ominous: "We'll have to wait a minute or two. Tom O'Daniels ain't here yet, and he's to do most of the talkin'."

Hardly had he finished, before the door opened and Tom O'Daniels pushed his way in. Tom was Irish and his bulldoggish face hadn't worn a genuine smile since the day he was saddled with Ira Peace's affairs. But he was smiling now — a broad grin that took away ten of his years. He stopped right there at the door and waved a fistful of papers, booming: "The meetin's over, gents. Ira's place was sold three minutes ago to a stranger by the name of Beauregard. You can all go home."

Thirty voices filled the room, wanting to know the particulars. Wiley banged for order, and his voice rose above the rest, gradually commanding silence: "Now I reckon I can tell you why we brought you up here. For two years this county's been sittin' on a case o' dynamite, waitin' for the lid to blow off. You all know what I mean.

11

Now, if Tom's right and Peace's outfit's been sold, we can all breathe easy and forget. . . ."

Wiley's voice droned on and on. A man standing alongside the door — a stoop-shouldered oldster with a tobacco-stained gray beard — quietly stepped out into the hall and started toward the stairs, his steps a little uncertain.

Pony Murdock's footsteps were always a little uncertain. Just now he was drunk. Rheumatism and a whiskey diet had long ago paralyzed his knee joints. As he strode, spraddle-legged, down the hall, his fists were jammed in his pockets and he was muttering angrily: "Beauregard. A damned Texan."

Pony was a bit disgusted, perhaps — disgusted that the makings of a good fight had temporarily been blown to the winds. Besides, he had long held Texans in contempt as Southern dandies. Their ways were too easy-going for old Pony who craved much excitement — and usually got it. "All they're good for is sittin' around talkin' and drinkin' soda pop with weeds in it," he snorted, hitching up his low-slung gun belt in which were holstered two old cap-and-ball .42s that Pony claimed beat anything Colt ever made. It was those guns that brought war to the Big Bend range.

Pony came to the stair head, thinking he'd go across to the saloon and finish his quart for the day. He started down the stairs, hands still in his pockets, when his boot heel caught on a frayed piece of the stair runner. He wasn't fast enough getting his hands out to make a grab at the banister. He fell forward, rolling onto one side, and, as his thigh smacked solidly on the third step below, the hammer of one of his low-slung guns was pried back and then fell as his weight eased away.

No one in the lobby below was watching the stairs, since most men were watching each other. When the hollow blast of that explosion sounded from above, the two crews lined facing each other across the lobby could think of only one thing — that the time for guns had come at last.

Fears's crew, to a man, reached for their holsters. And Major Hewes's riders, seeing that, made a frantic rush to get out of the way, only one of them drawing a weapon. He was foolish; before his front sight had cleared his belt, two guns across the room boomed out and his body jerked backward against the wall in two spasmodic jerks as the slugs took him.

Those two shots stopped the rest of the Broad Arrow crew on their way through the doors. They turned, saw their friend fall, and guns whipped out. The lobby was a shambles of smoke and deafening sound for a long half minute.

The two front windows were broken as men dived through and onto the porch. Someone tried to jump over the clerk's desk and it tipped over with a solid smash that scattered papers and ink and books out across the floor at the foot of the stairs.

When the smoke cleared, three Broad Arrow riders lay in their own blood before the front double doors. One Pitchfork man was down, moaning and clutching his stomach.

The room above cleared in ten seconds. Tom O'Daniels, the first man to the head of the stairs, looked down to see Pony Murdock picking himself painfully to his feet. He could also see a Broad Arrow man lying there by the door. The color left his face and he threw out his arms to stop those behind him.

"What happened, Pony?" he called down.

The oldster looked up at him, brushing off his soiled, worn clothes, feeling gingerly of a hurt elbow. He growled: "When you find out, let me know." Then he muttered something unintelligible, out of which clearly sounded the name Beauregard, and trudged out the front doors on his way across to the saloon.

O'Daniels turned and looked back over the heads of the men crowding behind. He spotted the sheriff and called: "You'd all better get back into that room! Wiley, take the major and Fears down the back way!"

Out front a girl stood directly across from the hotel. She had been standing there for nearly a minute now. She was pale, and she held a clenched hand to her mouth. She had heard those guns and seen the Broad Arrow riders run out of the doors a minute ago and pile into their saddles to race down the street. She had seen blood smearing one man's coat. Now, with the silence over at the hotel so prolonged as to be unbearable, she stepped down off the plank walk and started across the street.

A voice called out after her: "I wouldn't, miss!"

It was a pleasant, drawling voice. Above the panic that had taken hold of the girl, she felt more than a faint curiosity about the owner of that voice. She stopped, faced around, and saw a man step down off the walk and come toward her.

He was tall, and, when he smiled she instantly liked the warmth that was reflected in his gray eyes. That voice, along with those eyes, had a momentarily soothing effect on her. He touched the brim of his Stetson as he stopped a few feet away, and drawled: "Whatever it is, you can't help much."

But once again that panic mounted inside Gail Hewes. She had to know what had happened to her father, so she told the stranger shortly — "This isn't your affair." — and turned and started across once more.

Two quick steps put him alongside her, and he took her gently by the arm and cautioned: "There's more bullets where those came from. I'd hate to have you stop one."

She turned, jerked her arm away angrily, and all at once felt the hysteria that had been with her all this morning take hold. "And who are you to say what I should do?"

But his eyes weren't meeting hers any longer. He was looking on across the street, and her glance immediately followed his. A dozen men were coming down off the hotel steps, crossing the walk to their horses haltered at the hitching rail. They were Pitchfork men, Bill Fears's crew, and at sight of them Gail Hewes lost all control and ran across to the nearest.

"What have you done to Father?" she cried.

The rider took his foot out of the stirrup and faced her, a wry smile wreathing his

16

thin features. "Nothin', Miss Hewes. But that ain't sayin' what we will do."

"But Yace Hardy had blood on his coat when he came out!" she protested. "Where are the rest?"

The rider's smile broadened. "Lyin' in there waitin' to be measured for wooden underwear." He swung into the saddle, leaving the girl too stunned by his words to move or speak.

The Pitchfork crew wasted no time getting away. Yet they rode down the street at a trot, where Major Hewes's men had left at a dead run. In their going was a hint of the arrogance that always rode with the outfit.

Jim Beauregard, watching their departure from across the street, caught this difference between the two groups he had seen leave town within the last five minutes. Then he turned his attention toward the girl, who stood across there looking after Fears's crew with a stunned expression marring a face that was otherwise beautiful. He went across to her and said quietly: "I'd like to help."

"Who are you?" she asked quietly, facing him squarely now.

"Beauregard's the name . . . Jim Beauregard. I'm new here. This mornin' I bought myself a ranch."

A hint of suspicion edged into the girl's

hazel-eyed glance. She asked softly, breath-lessly: "Not Ira Peace's place?"

He nodded.

For five long seconds they stood there, motionless — except that a rigidity seemed to run through the girl's tall, willowy body. Suddenly she raised a hand and struck the stranger fully in the face.

His lips tightened into a thin line, and then he gave a bleak smile. "Women are dif-ferent up here," he drawled.

"You did it!" she breathed, an inward pas-sion finally reaching the breaking point. "Things were to be straightened out today. We could have lived in peace. And now you ride in here and destroy everything we've been working for!"

Beauregard's eyes had hardened, but his voice was calm enough as he queried: "I did it?"

"Of course you did! And I hate you!" All at once Gail Hewes choked back a sob and buried her face in her hands.

Nothing will make a man so uncomfort-able as to see a woman in tears. All the anger left Jim Beauregard, and he reached out and touched the girl on the arm, but she pulled away and raised her head.

"Don't touch me again!" she blazed. Then, hearing steps behind her, she turned and saw her father and Bill Fears, with Sheriff Wiley between them, come out of the passageway that ran between the hotel and the adjoining building. Not seeing her, they turned and started down the street in the direction of the jail.

She called — "Dad!" — and ran toward the trio.

Wiley waited until she stood before them, then said: "Now, Gail, you keep out of this. All I want is to get these two out of town without blowin' holes through each ether."

His voice carried so that Jim Beauregard heard it plainly. And he saw that the girl ignored the lawman, and heard her say: "Dad, what happened? Hardy had blood on his shirt and. . . ."

"I don't know what happened, Gail," Major Hewes answered quietly. "They didn't let me see." He turned to the sheriff and said harshly: "You can't arrest me, Wiley. I have my rights as a. . . ."

"Rights be damned, Major. I don't know any more about what happened than you. But I can guess, and, unless I get you two with half a county between you, you'll be at each other's throats before I turn my back." The butts of two guns hung out of one of the pockets of the sheriff's sheepskin, and Jim Beauregard now saw that the lawman's other prisoner wore an empty holster strapped low on his thigh.

"Then you can have my word for it I'll ride straight home," Major Hewes put in. "Hell, I have a right to know what that shootin' was about."

Bill Fears now spoke. "And I'll make the same promise, Wiley. You're makin' a play you can't back. I'll sue for false arrest."

The sheriff was plainly at a loss. He looked about him, half frantically, and finally growled: "I don't know why I should care what you do to each other. Go ahead, but I'll keep your irons. Fears, you ride out first."

Bill Fears, with his habitual, challenging smile, mockingly touched his flat-brimmed Stetson to the girl, and started to walk back along the walk. He was even with the steps of the hotel when he saw Jim Beauregard standing there by the hitch rail. He stopped, measured Beauregard with his glance for two long seconds, then said: "Welcome to Big Bend, stranger. So you're the Olive Branch's new owner?"

Instinct had guided Fears in his guess. He wasn't surprised to see the stranger nod, or to hear him say: "I'll take possession in about a week."

"If I had a gun on me, you'd never take

possession," Fears snarled, his smile gone now. "I suppose you started this thing?"

To see flaring hostility toward him ride the glance of a second person within the last few minutes, and again to be so wrongly accused of a part in something he did not even understand, galled Jim Beauregard. He didn't know what lay in back of the shooting, or how he was connected with it. But now, instead of a girl, a man faced him, and he didn't take that sort of talk from a man.

He stepped up onto the walk, reaching down to unbuckle the single belt that held the gun at his thigh. He swung it to one side, dropped it on the boards, and then stepped close in to Fears and drawled: "That gets rid of the gun."

Gail, her father, and Wiley were watching. The sheriff started to call out a warning, but, before he could speak, he saw Bill Fears's left fist lance out in a lightning stab.

That first blow caught Jim Beauregard fully on the point of the chin. It knocked him back into the hitch rail, snapping the pole. Had Fears's arm taken a full swing, the well-timed blow would have knocked a man unconscious. As it was, it momentarily stunned Beauregard. His lean body shifted its weight off the now broken tie rail. He moved with an ease that was deceptive, fast.

One moment his arms were hanging at his sides. The next, they had struck with a speed hard for the eyes to follow.

Wiley left Hewes and the girl and ran in to stop the fight. Someone came out onto the hotel porch and shouted, and others started to line the railing. It took Wiley perhaps five seconds to reach the pair. But he was too late. Fears was down on the walk, his face a smear of blood, his aquiline nose far off line and his lips puffed and bleeding. Jim Beauregard stood a few feet away, legs apart and rubbing a sprained hand, and, as Wiley came up, Beauregard drawled: "You're the first man that ever touched my face."

Wiley took him by the arm and pulled him away, growling: "There's been enough hell raised around here in one day. Lay off, stranger."

Beauregard didn't reply, but his gray eyes settled dangerously on the lawman, so that Wiley blurted out irritably: "I know you had a good reason. But I'll be damned if I'll see it go on." He turned, to see that Fears was getting to his feet, a little unsteadily. "You'd better ride, Bill."

Afterward, the few who had seen Fears's face just then remarked on his smile. It had all the wickedness and hate in the man's being concentrated in it. No one had ever before beaten Fears — in anything — and his nature wasn't a forgiving one. He didn't say a thing. He picked up his hat, reached into a pocket for a bandanna that he pressed to his lips, and then he was gone.

Wiley was getting the story of the fight in the hotel from one of the watchers, his hand still holding Beauregard's sleeve. The speaker was brief, concise: "Three of Hewes's riders shot to hell, Sheriff. Tade, Smith, and Shorty Crimp. Doc and Yace stopped lead and walked out bleedin'. Before they left, they got Harry Palls, and nicked Brady and Jeffers. Pony Murdock lit the match."

"What match?" Wiley asked.

"The one that blew the works. He fell down the stairs and his gun went off, accidental. No one knew what it was for about as long as the shake of a burro's tail. Then it was too late, and the guns were smokin'. This is sure hell."

"And that's what they're saddlin' on me?" Beauregard queried. "How come?"

Wiley looked up into this stranger's face, and sighed wearily: "That's a long story. But you'd better know it before we go any further. Step down to my office."

As they went on down the walk, two men

came out the doors carrying a limp body by shoulders and legs. Wiley stopped to look on, even shouted instructions: "Take him over to Moore's!"

Jim Beauregard was looking at Gail Hewes, seeing the tears that welled into her eyes at sight of her father's dead rider.

Major Hewes had his look at this stranger, said suddenly: "If I understand right, you're to be my neighbor. I apologize for the welcome we've given you."

"There's no apology needed," Beauregard answered. "Things happened pretty fast."

He was looking for the girl to unbend, as her father had. But Gail Hewes's glance didn't soften.

Just then Wiley turned and said: "You'd better be ridin', Major. I hate this about as bad as you do, but the thing to do now is to get out of town." He turned to Beauregard. "You come along with me, friend. I don't have much time, but I can tell you a thing or two."

II

Bill Fears wasn't the man to miss the chance of getting the county's sympathy. So he gave his single dead rider a funeral in town, with all the trimmings.

Major Hewes quietly buried his three men

24

in his own graveyard, on top of the knoll behind the Broad Arrow's sprawling stone ranch house. He had to bury Yace Hardy two days after that, for Hardy died finally from loss of blood on that long ride home after the shooting.

For the next ten days things were quiet. The major, much against his will, hired three new men, all hard-bitten strangers who wore their guns low and demanded high wages and got them.

The last of these, arriving one afternoon, announced briefly: "A bunch of Texas men hit town today."

The major didn't have his explanation of this until evening, shortly before sundown, when he saw Pony Murdock riding in along the trail.

Pony wasn't a man to command much respect. But he'd long been a friend of Major Hewes's, and the Broad Arrow owner was tolerant enough to excuse what Pony had done. Hewes waited on the porch for the oldster to dismount and climb the steps, and, when they stood face to face, Pony's glance wavered. He looked meekly at Gail, standing in the doorway behind her father, then at Hewes, and said lamely: "Major, I'll eat a pack o' dust and crawl back to town on my hands and knees, if that'll do any good."

"It won't, Pony. We know you're sorry."

Pony's glance brightened instantly. He sighed his relief. "I didn't know but what you'd put a bounty on my scalp." Then a shrewd look flashed into his eyes, and he queried: "Have you heard the news?"

The major shook his head.

"About the Texas men?" Pony asked.

"I've heard they're in town. Who are they?"

"This new feller, Beauregard, brought 'em in. All forkin' double-rigged hulls and wearin' bull-hide pants." Pony's tone was abusive in the extreme.

"Texas men all come double-rigged and wearing bull-hide chaps. They have to, coming from a country of brush and cactus. You say they're signin' on with Beauregard?"

Pony Murdock nodded. "Six of 'em. Have you heard what this Beauregard's doin'?" He didn't wait for an answer, but went on: "He hasn't bought the Olive Branch. What he did was pay good money for an option to buy within two years. I got that straight from Tom O'Daniels. And that's not all. He's tryin' a new game. It seems he's gathered a little money trail-bossin' herds comin' up from Texas to Dodge and Abilene. This year he bought up all the culls he could lay hands on . . . the critters left over after shippin' season was finished. He's havin' close onto three thousand driven down here, onto his range, and aims to winter the bunch and sell 'em at a profit next summer."

"It's been done before," the major said. "Sometimes a man can make a lot of money at it. Beauregard's smart."

"Smart!" Pony snorted derisively. "What chance has he got beddin' down between two . . . ?" He broke off in time, his face flushed a little in embarrassment. "I'm not one to say. But he'll bear watchin'."

"Hold your horses, Pony. You can't condemn a man for trying his hand at something."

Pony Murdock was plainly surprised. He had ridden out here expecting to find support for his views on this new Beauregard — he couldn't find it in town, for everyone seemed to like the newcomer — and now the major wasn't coming around the way he'd thought he would. If the major hadn't said — "Come in and wet your whistle, Pony." — the oldster would have climbed back in his saddle and headed for town. As it was, he licked his lips and followed his friend into the spacious main room of the house, pointedly ignoring Gail Hewes's rather belittling glance.

Gail and her father disagreed on this one point — Pony's fondness for alcohol — the major claiming that you can't teach an old dog new tricks and that the best thing to do is to keep him at the ones he knows best. So, whenever Pony Murdock showed at the Broad Arrow, he had at least one drink of the major's fine bourbon. Gail didn't like it.

Pony stayed for supper that night. He was there when three Broad Arrow riders came pounding into the yard, one of them weaving in the saddle and his face covered with blood, and all three broncos badly blown and lathered.

The major and Gail and Pony all heard them arrive, and they went out onto the porch and saw the commotion down by the bunkhouse as other members of the crew helped the wounded man out of the saddle and carried him inside.

Pony was close behind the major all the way to the bunkhouse. Hewes asked the first man he met — "Something wrong?" — and got the answer: "Bill Reed's shot up a bit. Agate is in there tellin' about it now."

Inside the bunkhouse Agate Belden, telling his story to the others, broke off and began again: "Major, hell's busted loose!"

He glanced at Gail in apology for his profanity. "There were seven of 'em caught us at the north end of the river pasture, while we were ridin' up to fix that fence. There isn't much cover up there, and they had to throw their lead from quite a ways off, otherwise we'd all be coyote feed by now. We rode out of there fast, cuttin' up onto the barrancas before we pulled in. From up there we looked back and saw what they did. They must have been gatherin' all afternoon, for they had a bunch of two, maybe three hundred critters waitin' in a draw off there to the east. As soon as we hightailed, they worked 'em in toward the river. And they drove every damned steer down over that high bank! They're piled up there now, not a blessed one left alive! They had to shoot the last few."

The major didn't speak. Neither did the rest. Gail Hewes's face went white, the pallor of her skin accentuated by the burnished copper of her chestnut hair. Pony Murdock swallowed thickly, tried to speak and couldn't.

Finally Agate broke the awesome silence. "If we'd had a glass, we might have spotted one or two. As it was, they were too far away. I didn't even recognize any of their jugheads. If they hadn't put a slug through

Reed's shoulder, we'd have gone back and done a little powder-burnin'. As it was, Reed was bleedin' bad and we had to get him in here."

"What time did it happen?" the major asked quietly.

"Just before sundown. It didn't take long, maybe twenty minutes."

"You all right, Reed?" Hewes went over to the bunk where his rider lay, and looked down at him.

Bill Reed smiled and said: "Sure, Major." Then, as an afterthought: "Hell, Major, that was a hard thing to watch. All those critters pilin' up over that cliff. I . . . ." Words failed him and he locked his jaw and glared his hatred for the men who had brought this disaster to the Broken Arrow.

"I know," Hewes said. He turned to his men. "It looks like we'll have to throw a guard around our fence. Agate, you take four men and drive in that North Fork bunch. They're too far away to watch. Throw them into the creek pasture. The rest of you take turns along the fence. And you'd better carry your Winchesters."

He looked from man to man, and saw only one thing mirrored in their unwavering glances — a hatred that was white-hot.

He walked to the door, and was about to

go out. All at once a man behind cleared his throat and said — "Major!" — and Hewes stopped and faced around again. The speaker was Jeff Bates, one of Agate's companions who had ridden in a few minutes ago. He was a trifle embarrassed now, and shifted his feet nervously as he glanced warily across at the wounded rider. "Agate won't like what I'm goin' to say, because he says I didn't see it. But I've got good eyes and sometimes I can see a thing or two others can't. I . . . I. . . ."

"Get on with it, Jeff," the major put in.

"Well, it's just this. I'd swear on a Bible that those jaspers were ridin' double-rigged hulls."

"And I say you couldn't see that far," Agate protested.

The major didn't speak for long, tense moments, considering soberly the implications of this news. Finally, looking at Jeff, he said: "If they were double-rigged, you've got the idea they were these Texans, Beauregard's men?"

Jeff's face was flushed, and he was obviously uncomfortable. "I won't label any man with that job. This Beauregard seems to be white. But" — his jaw shelved out obstinately — "I can still swear those gents' hulls were double-rigged."

"We'll think about it," the major said, and left.

Pony, walking on one side of the major, Gail on the other, waited for what they knew was coming. Finally, as they climbed onto the porch, Hewes said almost inaudibly: "He couldn't be the man."

"Major, you're gettin' soft!" Pony exploded. "Why in tarnation hell couldn't it be this Beauregard? He's just a Texas polecat!"

"Easy on your words," the major said sharply. "Pony, you'll keep this under your hat. There's a law in this country and I aim to use it. I'll get Wiley out here tomorrow and we can go at this thing like two sane men. My guess would be that Bill Fears is in back of it. But there again, it's only a guess."

Pony was too mad to speak. He snorted his disgust, turned, and stomped down off the steps and straight across to his haltered horse. He climbed into the saddle, his back stiff with pride, and rode out of the yard.

Gail, who had been silent up until now, couldn't help but smile. "He's a lovable old fool." Then, more seriously: "Why couldn't Beauregard have done this, Dad?"

"I know my men, and Jim Beauregard hasn't what it takes to do a thing like this."

She sighed, not knowing in her own mind what to think, and went on inside and to her room. Many times these last few days she'd thought of Jim Beauregard and hated herself for the way her thoughts turned. She couldn't forget his smile, his strong, aquiline face, and those calm gray eyes, and, when she remembered the gentle but firm touch of his hand on her arm, she hated herself for the thrill that set her heart to pounding. So she had schooled herself to a grim dislike for him.

She reasoned this way: if he hadn't bought Peace's Olive Branch, the meeting wouldn't have ended in such disorder, and Pony Murdock wouldn't have fallen down the stairs and started all this. Once or twice she felt ashamed of herself for so indirectly settling the blame on this newcomer's shoulders. Was it his fault that the mere circumstance of his coming had loosed all these time-aged passions? Yes, she wanted to believe it was. So she wouldn't let herself have any contradictory thoughts.

Pony Murdock knew what he had to do, and he was the man to do it. At heart, he wasn't brave, but whiskey will do strange things to a man, and, so long as Pony felt the warmth of that bracer in his guts, he was stubborn. He rode straight to the Olive

Branch, arriving in a little more than an hour. He knew the layout, and, as the shadowed buildings rose up out of the darkness ahead, he had a faintly friendly feeling toward the men who lived there; during Ira Peace's time he had grown fond of it.

But he put down that feeling and made straight for the long frame wing that jutted out from the far end of the square, weathered house. Ira Peace had used that wing as his bunkhouse, and doubtless this Beauregard was doing the same. Pulling in squarely in front of the door, he stayed in the saddle and bawled out lustily: "Beauregard! Beauregard, get the hell out here!"

The door swung open, and Jim Beauregard's tall shape was outlined in it. Behind him, Pony could see a room blue with smoke, a big round table ringed by the Texas men he'd seen earlier that day in town. Two chairs were empty, and that bothered Pony.

Beauregard, after a two second wait in which his eyes searched the darkness outside, drawled: "Oh, so it's you, Murdock. Light down, and come in."

Pony wasn't getting down. The longer he sat there, the braver he felt. At length he said: "You thought you got off without bein' seen, eh? But you're wrong. The whole damn' pack o' you will be in jail by mornin'!"

Beauregard took two steps out from the door. Even though his face was shadowed, Pony could see that he frowned as he said: "You're drunk, Murdock."

Pony was through talking. His right hand was resting on his thigh, and it was less than four inches to his gun. He didn't move that hand fast, yet it didn't take long to palm out his gun, either. He was raising it into line, thumbing back the hammer. Suddenly, off to his left, the night was lit by a small orange burst of flame. At the same time as he heard the sharp explosion of a rifle shot, Pony felt his hand jerked by a powerful blow that tore the heavy .42 from his grasp. The gun spun far out and lit with a *thud*, kicking up a little gray cloud of dust. Pony's hand was numb from the shock, but unhurt.

Beauregard called out — "Nice shot, Charley!" — and walked over and picked up Pony's gun. He looked across at the oldster who was too scared to speak and said: "Get down and come in and tell your story. You should have known I'd have this place guarded."

Pony wasn't getting down, for his nerve was retreating with the passing of each long second. He wasn't getting down — until

Beauregard all at once turned his own gun on him and said quietly: "Maybe you didn't hear, Murdock."

The oldster had seen a man or two knocked off his feet by one of the bullets from that old cap-and-ball pistol. He wasn't sure but what one of the slugs could lift a man right out of the saddle. So he swung to the ground, even took the precaution of holding his hands at the level of his ears as he crossed the yard, and went in the door. Beauregard was plainly a man who wasn't to be played with.

Inside, five Texans looked across at Pony as he came through the door. On the table lay stacks of chips and a heap of cards. The men weren't hostile; instead, their glances showed a thinly veiled amusement.

Jim Beauregard shut the door behind him and tossed Pony's old six-gun onto the table. "Now let's have it. You say we'll be in jail by mornin'?"

Pony Murdock had talked his way out of some tight places. The years had schooled his expressions, his mannerisms until it was said that to know what the oldster was thinking a man would have to be a mind-reader. Just now Pony's wrinkled old face relaxed into a broad grin and he croaked: "Can't you gents take a joke? I just stopped in for a drink."

Beauregard said shortly: "George, give Murdock a drink." He stood there and waited calmly while one of the Texans reached back into a bunk and brought out a bottle and poured half a tumbler of whiskey into a glass. Then he picked up the glass and handed it to Pony, and stood there while Pony drank the liquor, every last drop of it.

When Pony had set the glass down on the table and wiped his drooping mustache with the back of his hand, Beauregard drawled: "You were sayin' somethin' about us all goin' to jail."

The tone, the man's manner, and the ominous meaning behind those words shattered Pony's nerve. He blurted out his whole story, and no man interrupted. Finished, he took the nearest vacant chair and reached for his bandanna to wipe the sweat off his brow, dead certain he wouldn't get out alive. All at once Jim Beauregard laughed, long and quietly, even his gray eyes mirroring his amusement. He walked around to the far side of the table and took the other vacant chair, and, when he was sitting, his look was once more serious. He said: "Murdock wants to buy into the game. Deal a hand, Charley. And set that bottle where he can reach it."

So Pony, much against his will, bought into the game. At first he was nervous, wondering how long it would be before they picked an excuse to put a bullet through him. Several times he took a long pull at the bottle; no one seemed to mind. Finally the bottle was empty and another took its place. Pony's fears left him.

These Texans were the right sort. None of them made any attempt to deny that they had raided the Broad Arrow, yet, as the time went on, Pony was certain they hadn't done it. And he didn't know why he felt that way.

Shortly before midnight the game ended. When Pony, drunk and drowsy, got up to leave, Beauregard said: "We turned your bronc' loose in the corral. Maybe you ought to bed down here for the night."

Pony nodded, thankful he wasn't having to make that twelve-mile ride home. Then he caught Jim Beauregard's shrewd glance on him. Jim said: "That herd of mine will be pullin' in any day now. I'll need a couple more riders. You know any I could hire, Pony?"

The oldster thought a moment or two, then had a brilliant idea. Before he knew what he was doing, he had said: "It's been years since I worked. But there was a time when they called me a top hand. I'd like one of those jobs."

"We're a bunch o' Texas jaspers, Pony," Beauregard reminded him.

Pony grinned sheepishly. "Maybe I've been wrong all along about that. I still want that job."

III

The Olive Branch crew had its hands full for the next week. 3,400 head of longhorns were pushed onto the range, and it was day and night work for Beauregard's men to keep the critters quiet and get them used to their new grass.

The word came out that the sheriff had made no progress in his hunt for the parties responsible for the raid on Major Hewes's herd. The major himself stopped at the Olive Branch late one afternoon and had a talk with Beauregard. Pony, watching from the bunkhouse — yet keeping out of the major's sight, because he was half ashamed to be found there — thought that the two men seemed uncommonly friendly.

The next morning Beauregard sent for Pony and told him they were going into town. The two of them rode down Bend City's main street shortly before eleven, and, surprisingly enough, Beauregard swung in at the hitch rail in front of the jail.

Pony frowned. "You goin' in there?"

Beauregard nodded, and climbed from the saddle.

"I'll wait," Pony said. He and Wiley hadn't been such good friends since the hotel shooting.

Beauregard said — "Come along. I'll want you to hear this." — and started across the walk. Pony reluctantly followed.

Inside the sheriff's office, Wiley was already talking to Beauregard. The sheriff looked at Pony, scowled slightly, and turned to Beauregard again. "So you're beginnin' to lose a few critters?"

Beauregard nodded. "Not a few. At least a hundred and fifty head. And I know where they went."

Pony couldn't understand this. Nothing had been said about rustlers out at the bunkhouse; these Texans were a close-mouthed outfit.

But if this discovery surprised Pony, what Beauregard said next was like a breathtaking body blow. "Two days ago I followed the sign of a small bunch five miles onto Pitchfork range. I reckon it was a foolish move. A gent with a rifle didn't like it." Beauregard lifted his right arm and ran a finger through a hole in the side of his shirt.

"That's how close he came."

Sheriff Wiley's face lost a shade of color. His shaggy brows gathered in a look of bafflement, and he muttered: "So it's Bill Fears, after all."

Beauregard moved his wide shoulders in a shrug. "I didn't get far enough to find the proof. I'm tellin' you only what happened."

"And what do you want me to do about it? I don't like Bill Fears any better than you, but namin' a man a rustler is askin' for trouble. Why would Fears do it?"

"That's a question I can't answer. It'll suit me if you keep this to yourself. I didn't come in to ask any help from the law. Only I wanted you to know what's shapin' up . . . in case anything happens."

"Beauregard," Wiley snapped abruptly, "do you think Fears's bunch made that raid on the Broad Arrow two weeks ago?"

"It's hard to see why they would. And it's still harder to see why they'd take a likin' to my beef."

Wiley shook his head. "No, for a man who's lived in this country it's not hard to see why Fears wants your place. He'd like to wind up havin' all the Big Bend range under his brand. That's my private opinion. But we can't pin anything on him." Wiley stood up, jammed his hands in his pockets, and began pacing back and forth behind his desk. "I'd give a lot if you hadn't turned up. So long as Ira Peace's outfit was bein' run by the court, Fears couldn't make a move. He may have rustled a little of the major's beef, but that didn't mean much. The main thing is that before you came, your layout kept those two curly wolves from each other's throats. Now that's all changed. . . ."

He was about to go on, but just then the door opened and a man stepped in — a thick-set individual who wore a deputy sheriff's badge on his coat. He slammed the door with a crash that matched the excitement on his face. "Wiley, there's a herd of South Texas longhorns five miles the other side of the crossin'."

"South Texas?" Wiley echoed. Abruptly his look hardened. "How are the papers?"

"They ain't got any. I had a look at a few hundred up at the point of the herd. They're a sick-lookin' bunch?"

"The fever?"

The deputy shrugged. "I ain't no doctor, but it'll be plain hell around here if they are carriers. I had a talk with the owner . . . Ransom's his name . . . and told him he ought to stay on the west bank of the river and swing wide of our range. He won't listen. It seems he's fillin' an Indian contract

42

for delivery at Fort Reeder. He's late, and he claims he'll lose fifty miles unless he crosses at Boulder Ford."

Wiley rammed his Stetson onto his grizzled head, strapped a second shell belt and gun on his left thigh, lifted a rifle off the back behind his desk, and growled: "We'll go see this Ransom."

At the door, he paused, and turned to say to Beauregard — "Let me know if I can help." — and went out.

Beauregard and Pony sat there a moment, considering this news. South Texas cattle were known to be carriers of Texas fever. The animals, apparently healthy, when thrown in with another herd, could spread the fever like wildfire. Whole herds had been wiped out in this way, until now every town along the cattle trails to the north watched the incoming drives and would stop and turn back any herds from south of the imaginary line that had been drawn across the state of Texas, the quarantine line.

"The fever's a damn' funny thing," Pony said. "Once I was ridin' for an outfit bringin' a herd across from northern New Mexico. We cut the fresh sign of a big bunch one day. Ten days later our critters took sick. In another week we didn't have enough alive to butcher a good meal for the crew. Seems their innards dry up, their backs crack open, they can't get enough water. Wouldn't that be a nice thing to have hit our range, along with this other trouble?"

Beauregard was looking out the window, watching a group of riders trotting down the street, on their way toward the center of town. "There goes Bill Fears and his bunch," he announced.

Pony stepped to the window, looked out, and caught a glimpse of Fears riding a sleek chestnut, and growled derisively: "He sits his hull mighty proud." He chuckled softly. "From here it looks like he rubbed some coal dust under that right eye. It couldn't be your label, could it, Jim?"

So far as Pony could tell, Beauregard hadn't heard. All he said was: "He's a hard man to figure." Shortly he straightened and came up out of his chair. "Let's get down to the hardware store and order that wire."

The north line of fence that separated the Olive Branch's range from that of the Pitchfork was badly in need of repair. Beauregard had put off ordering new wire, in hopes that the old fence would do. But now, with a bunch of longhorns that would push over a fence and leave if they could, he wasn't taking chances. That morning he had told his crew that they were to start work on that five-mile-long fence the next day.

They left the sheriff's office and walked toward the town's center, leaving their horses at the jail tie rail. Up ahead, Fears and his riders were dismounting in front of the hotel.

Beauregard placed his order at the hardware store, arranged for a wagon to bring out his load of wire. He was finished, putting his receipt in a pocket of his Levi's, when Pony abruptly stepped in close behind him and nudged him in the back, muttering: "Here comes trouble."

Beauregard turned to face the front of the store, in time to see Bill Fears and two of his riders come in the doors.

Fears looked back along the aisle between the counters, feigning surprise, and said levelly: "This is luck." He came on back, and finally stopped ten feet away, his men behind him. "I'm packin' an iron today, Beauregard."

The threat was so open that no man would have ignored it. Beauregard didn't. In the one flashing sideward glance Pony Murdock took at his boss, he saw Jim's aquiline face set in a broad, disarming grin.

Then Jim Beauregard drawled: "You're packin' two irons, friend Fears. Down in our country men don't wear a pair o' guns.

One's enough."

"This isn't your country," Fears rasped. It was the first time Pony Murdock could remember not seeing the man smile. "You asked for this, Beauregard."

As Fears spoke, his two hands were already streaking toward the sagging holsters at his thighs. Behind him his men lunged to one side, out of the line of fire. Pony took a sideward step, too, wondering whether or not to go for his guns.

But suddenly, hands locked on gun butts, Fears's lightning move froze. Pony's head swiveled around and he saw, with amazement, that Jim Beauregard's single .45 was already out, lined at Fears.

"For a man that makes big talk, you're almighty slow, Fears," Beauregard said, his voice low and drawling. Abruptly his gun flicked over in his palm and settled back into its holster. "Like to try it again?"

Fears hadn't had the time to take his hands from the handles of his guns. As Beauregard's taunting words whipped out at him, his two arms tensed and he lifted his weapons clear, in frantic haste.

Yet, before Pony's awed gaze, Beauregard's hand again flashed upward and out, the motion timed to one smooth flow of muscle. His draw caught Fears with guns half raised. Again the Pitchfork owner hesitated, even winced at the expected bullet.

In some way, Bill Fears had gained the reputation of being fast on the draw. Yet here was a man who had given him the advantage twice, and still had beaten him. It was a hard thing for a man to watch, harder yet for Bill Fears to find himself so powerless.

If he had raised those weapons another inch, he would have been a dead man. He didn't raise them. Instead, he slowly put them back in their open holsters and reached up to wipe the beaded perspiration from his brow. And his two men behind him, two prime examples of the killer crew that Fears had hired, were careful to keep their hands in sight.

Once more Jim Beauregard sheathed his .45. Once more he spoke in his soft drawl: "Again, friend?"

Fears's square face flushed under the stinging taunt. For a tense second it looked as though his temper would snap, that he was signing his own death certificate. But finally, with obvious effort, he turned on his heel and without a word walked out the front doors. His men followed.

Pony Murdock felt like shouting. Inside him glowed a warmth of feeling that wouldn't bear putting into words. He had lived a long and full life, yet never before had he seen a thing like this. Jim Beauregard, quiet, minding his own business, could have beaten any man Pony had ever known, and he'd known more gunfighters than he could count.

He said — "Jim, that was worth seein'." — and, when Beauregard started toward the door, he walked proudly at his side.

There was a group at the foot of the hotel steps — Fears's crew — that eyed them with grudging respect as they passed along the opposite walk. When they were a little way beyond, Pony glanced over his shoulder and said: "My back's crawlin'."

Beauregard laughed softly. "Fears wouldn't make a play like that . . . not here in town."

Neither spoke again until they were a full mile out on the trail. It was then that Pony mumbled an oath and said: "How in hell do you do it, Jim? That cutter o' yours . . . why, a man couldn't even see it leave leather."

"Luck, Pony."

"Luck, hell! It's magic. Jim, we're in for trouble." Beauregard didn't deny the assertion. And because he didn't, Pony was really worried.

■ ■ ■ ■

Yesterday, Gail Hewes had listened to her father's story of his talk with Jim Beauregard. When he finished, she had admitted: "I was wrong about him."

Her father had nodded. "You were wrong, so was Pony. He's signed on with the Olive Branch crew."

Perhaps that was the thing that convinced her — Beauregard's making a friend of Pony Murdock. She was secretly happy, for now that she cast aside all her prejudices, she realized she'd wanted to like this stranger from the beginning.

This morning she had said to her father: "Why don't we ask our neighbor over for supper tonight?" And he'd agreed that it was a good idea. The amused look that had flashed in his brown eyes as he did so was a bit embarrassing, but Gail had ignored it.

So now, as she rode down off the slope and across the floor of the broad valley toward the Olive Branch ranch house, she was looking forward to this meeting with Beauregard. She had purposely waited until late in the afternoon — it was now almost five — so that, if he accepted her invitation, he would have to ride back with her.

At the house, a soft-speaking Texan told her: "You're half an hour too late, Miss Hewes. Jim rode out to make a swing of that north fence."

Just then Pony Murdock appeared in the bunkhouse doorway. He grinned — a little sheepishly, Gail thought — and said: "So you've come around, too."

"Hello, Pony. Do you think you could help me find Jim?" She called him by his first name before she thought, and it was Pony's turn to look amused.

"We'll try," he told her. "Give me time to throw my hull onto a bronc'."

Later, as they swung west and into sight of the river, Pony announced: "Jim's worried. Some of our critters have taken a likin' for the other side of that fence. The only strange thing is that they cut the wire before they went through."

"Bill Fears?" she queried soberly.

Pony nodded. "Jim and Bill had a run-in in town today." His look all at once brightened. "Golly, girl, you should have been there to see! Fears went for his cutter, and twice Jim beat him as easy as. . . ."

His words trailed out into silence. He was looking off into the west, against the glare of the horizon-touching sun. He raised a hand to shade his eyes against the strong light.

The girl said impatiently: "Go on, Pony. What happened?"

But Pony didn't hear. Now, following his glance, she looked out across the mile-distant winding river and saw a faraway thick fog of dust just below the horizon, miles back from the opposite bank.

"What is it, Pony?"

He looked at her once more. "That'll be that South Texas herd the sheriff rode out to turn away this mornin'." And he went on to tell her about the herd headed for Fort Reeder, about Texas fever and what it would mean if the disease ever got a toehold on the Big Bend range. "But I reckon it won't," he added. "They're still on the other side o' the river and they can't make a crossin' within the next fifty miles. Wiley must have told 'em off, and made it stick."

Pony was wrong. Two miles farther on, as the light failed and dusk settled quickly across the rolling sweep of range dotted by small bunches of cattle, Gail reined in. "I'd better go back. It's too late to find Jim now. Suppose you tell him to come over tomorrow night instead?"

She was plainly disappointed, and didn't want Pony to see. So she turned away as

51

she spoke, looking off into the west. They had been following the rim of a low ridge that skirted the line of the river a quarter mile away. Now, 100 feet higher than the banks of the stream, she could look down directly on it, and this dying light seemed to bring far objects out in startling clarity.

Pony was saying — "I'm sorry about that. But he'll be along tomorrow." — when Gail saw the two riders a few hundred yards beyond the far bank of the river.

"Who could that be?" she asked Pony, raising a hand to point out the riders.

When he spotted them, Pony frowned. The west bank of Bull River was for miles a sandy, grassless waste that had never been used for ranching. "It might be a couple riders from that trail herd crew," he muttered. But suddenly he caught his breath and swore half audibly. "Take a look across there now. Some critters just climbed out of that draw ahead of that pair."

Gail saw them then, four long-horned steers plodding along ahead of the riders. Once one of the steers tried to cut back toward the west, but immediately the nearest rider spurred out and brought the animal back into line.

Gail had lost interest. She wheeled her bay around and said: "Be sure you tell Jim."

"Hold on!" Pony said excitedly. "Don't you want to see what happens?"

"Why should I?"

Pony's glance was still on the riders. "Don't that look strange to you? No cattle feed for a good forty miles the other side across there. And there's nothin' to bring a man ridin' in there. Yet there they are. And they're comin' this way."

Even as he spoke, one rider cut out and swung the lead steer in toward the river. In another minute the pair was pushing the steers down over the high-sloping riverbank, heading them for the water.

"I reckon I'll get along and see what happens," Pony growled.

All at once Gail understood. "They're from the trail herd," she breathed, her voice catching in her throat. "And they're coming across onto Jim's range. Pony, it couldn't be that!"

"But it is," he muttered, as he rammed spurs into his horse's flanks.

She followed, all at once afraid. The light was failing fast now, and the darkness came on quickly. Pony was riding at a slow walk, listening, keeping to cover whenever he could find it. By the time they reached the riverbank, it was so dark that they couldn't see clearly more than fifty feet ahead. Pony stopped. They sat there for a full half minute, neither of them moving.

Abruptly, from upstream, they heard a sound of splashing, then a man's sharp cry.

"That'll be them," Pony muttered, and moved off into the darkness. Gail saw that one of his cap-and-ball pistols rested across his saddle horn.

Pony would go on twenty yards at a time, then stop and sit looking sharply into the impenetrable shadows ahead. Once they both pulled up short as they heard a second loud splashing in the stream. The sound died out, then came again, farther away. A few seconds later the mutter of hoofs striking the hard-packed ground shuttled across from the far bank.

Pony let the breath out of his lungs in a gusty sigh. "They're gone. Now we've got a job ahead, findin' those steers."

It took them twenty minutes, and, when they did finally locate the four strange steers, it was to find them bunched with ten Olive Branch animals. They bore a broad Double B brand on the hide of their rumps.

Pony said: "I'll need help. We'll have to drive this whole bunch a mile or so north. There's an arroyo up there that cuts out of a small box draw. We can run 'em in there and pile brush across the mouth. They'll have water in there, too."

"But why go to all this trouble?" Gail protested. "Why not cut them out and drive them back across the river?"

"Jim'll want proof," was Pony's reply. "I aim to see that he gets it. We'll know in a week."

Gail forgot that she was already late for supper. She helped Pony work the bunch of steers north along the line of the river, and then into a grassy draw perhaps two acres in area. It suited Pony's purpose nicely, the sides being steep and rocky so that the animals couldn't climb out the mouth, a high-banked arroyo, less than twenty feet across, and at the far end a spring welled out of the gravelly bank and formed a shallow pool that would give the animals all the water they needed.

When the last steer had jogged heavily through the opening and into the draw, Pony said: "Now you get on home. I'll stay here and drag some brush to keep 'em in. And let's keep this under our hats until we know for sure. There's plenty of time to tell Jim, but when we do, I want to give him the whole story."

"He ought to know now," Gail said.

Pony shook his head. "I started all this trouble, and, maybe with luck, I can help finish it. Let me have my way this time, Gail. Not a word to Jim until I say so."

She agreed reluctantly, and a minute later headed for the Broad Arrow. Pony worked for better than an hour, until the mouth of the arroyo was choked with a five-foot wall of brush he had dragged up from the river-bank.

When he left the place, Pony didn't head back for the bunkhouse. Instead, he spurred his roan into the muddy waters of Bull River and swam him across to the opposite bank. By midnight he was within sight of the fires of the trail herd camp.

IV

The next afternoon Gail worked in the kitchen for two hours with Mike, the Chinese cook. Mike's cooking of plain food was already legend on the Big Bend, but tonight Gail was to serve a meal that would be long remembered. Two years before a friend of Major Hewes's had shipped out half a dozen country hams from Kentucky. There was one left, the largest, and Gail took it out of the winter cellar at noon and personally supervised its preparation and baking.

But Jim Beauregard didn't come for supper that night. Gail and her father waited until long after dark before they sat down to the table. The food seemed tasteless to Gail; she was disappointed and angry. The major complimented his daughter on her cooking, but, getting no response, he finished the meal in silence. Gail went to her room early.

For the next ten days she was quiet, seldom out of the house. Major Hewes, accustomed to seeing his daughter up and out early for a ride each morning, thought he understood the signs. Gail was in love. Once or twice he mentioned Jim Beauregard, and each time she gave him a short answer.

On the eleventh day, at breakfast, noticing Gail's lack of color and appetite, the major said: "You ought to ride over and see him."

"See who?" Gail asked with great indifference.

"Beauregard. Maybe he's sick . . . or hurt."

Color drained out of Gail's face. "I hadn't thought of that," she said, her voice barely audible. She got up from the table, changed her dress to a pair of man's Levi's and a wool jacket, and ten minutes later was riding out the trail that led north toward the Olive Branch.

Jim Beauregard was the first man she saw as she rode in toward the house. He sat the top pole of the big corral up by the barn. Someone pointed her out to him, and he swung down and strode across the bare yard toward her. Seeing him in such obvious good health and catching his open smile was irritating in the extreme.

She didn't get out of the saddle, and, before he had the time to speak, she was saying: "We had old country ham, fried chicken, and strawberry preserves. Mike made some Dutch cheese, and there were potatoes, beets, and radishes from the garden, and. . . ."

"And why wasn't I invited?" he interrupted politely.

"You were." His five words had somehow changed everything. "Or were you? Where's Pony?"

Jim shrugged. "Gone. This quiet life out here didn't seem to agree with him."

"Gone? Where?"

"We don't know. He hasn't been in his bunk for over a week."

As she lifted her foot out of the stirrup and stepped to the ground, a rising alarm was running through her. "Then he didn't come home a week ago Tuesday? He didn't tell you that we wanted you over for supper the next night?"

Beauregard shook his head soberly. "He didn't. And I take it you had a real feed." His hint of a smile became a frown. "Has something happened to Pony?"

Instead of answering directly, Gail said: "There's something you ought to see. It's down by the river. Can you ride out there with me?"

It took him less than three minutes to go to the corral and throw a saddle on a slim-legged buckskin.

As they rode around the barn and cut out across the pasture behind, Gail told her story. When she was halfway through it, Jim reined his buckskin out of its walk and into a trot, and, when she finished, he put the animal to a stiff run, and she had all she could do to keep up with him.

She couldn't find the spot where they had left the bunch of steers, but when she told Beauregard what she was looking for he led the way half a mile north along the low ridge that flanked the river. They were above the spot when he pulled in, looking down into the draw. Gail's glance held for two sickening seconds before she looked away.

"Pony was right," Beauregard breathed.

Four steers — the four South Texas animals — were on their feet and grazing at the far end of the draw, close into the pile of brush that choked the mouth. But directly below, ringing the muddy shallow pool, were the carcasses of the ten Olive Branch steers. It wasn't a pleasant sight, and Beauregard turned away.

"Those four critters would have wiped me out," he said. "I'll send a couple of men in here with coal oil and rifles. We'll shoot those four and burn all the carcasses."

"And what about Pony?"

Beauregard didn't answer for a long moment. At length he sighed wearily. "Who knows? We'd better be ridin' back."

He had no word to say on that long four-mile ride. Before she left him, she said: "My invitation's still good. Can you come to supper tonight?"

"I'd rather wait a day or two."

She knew what he meant without asking, and, as she rode out of the yard, she was remembering the grim set of his face, the absence of his smile. Halfway home, a panic gripped her. She felt instinctively that Jim Beauregard was headed into danger. She had to talk to someone, so she hurried home and told her father the whole story.

Half an hour later he drove the buckboard away from the wagon shed, after telling her that he was on his way in to see the sheriff.

Back at the Olive Branch, Beauregard called in three men working broncos down at the corral; the rest of the crew — three more — were finishing the work on the north fence.

When the trio stood in his office, he told them briefly what had happened, and ended by saying: "So we know Pony's in trouble. Red, you go up and get the others. Tonight, after it's dark, five of you will get on up to the Pitchfork and be on hand in case you're needed. Leave one man here to watch the place."

"And where'll you be?" Red, the youngest of the three, asked.

"I don't know yet. I'll ride up along the river and see what sign I can pick up." Beauregard spoke tersely, and his manner impressed the others with the full seriousness of Pony's disappearance.

"If any one of you wants to head out of this, now's the time." Jim paused, but all he saw on the faces of his listeners was a grim resolve that matched his own. So he went on: "I've ridden Pitchfork range, nights mostly, and I know a little about it. Two miles to the east of the house there's a stretch of broken country where you can hide. Two men watching the layout at one time will be enough. Take turns, day and night, and you might take along those glasses of mine. Don't light a fire. You'd better cook up a lot of grub this afternoon and pack it in with you. If anything happens down there that looks suspicious, you're to surround the place and stop anyone comin' out. If there's shootin', do what you think best."

A silence followed his words until one man said: "If we're two miles away, it'll take a long time to ride in."

"Then leave your horses in the brakes and fort up as close in to the layout as you can." Beauregard had turned and was filling his pockets with .30-30 shells from a box on the table behind him. "One more thing," he added. "Unless you have to, don't shoot to kill . . . not unless you see either me or Pony down there."

Ten minutes later he had cut out a fresh horse, a short-coupled black, and was riding off toward the river again. Red had already left to bring in the rest from the north fence.

Beauregard picked up Pony's sign a few rods north of the mouth of the draw and followed it to the river's edge. He swam his horse across the stream and found the sign on the other side. Two miles farther on, he lost it in the broad swath of churned earth that was the mark of the trail herd. He followed that, north and east.

An hour short of sundown he saw a moving speck crawl above the sage-studded horizon ahead. It was Pony Murdock. Even at a distance it was evident that Pony was drunk. He was riding at a walk, reins looped over the saddle horn, both hands clutching the saddle swells to hold him steady. His roan stopped of its own accord twenty feet short of Beauregard, and Pony jerked up his head. He blinked his red-rimmed eyes and his wrinkled old face broke into a grin.

"Damned if it ain't!" he said thickly. "Hi, yuh, Jim!"

"Howdy, Pony. Been away to see the sights?"

"Sights! I been away. . . ." Pony's voice broke off, and suddenly a look of cunning came to his eyes. When he went on, his voice was pitched to a lower key and he raised his right hand and wagged a blunt forefinger. "Jim, leave everything to me. I got somethin' to show you that will blow this damned thing higher'n a kite."

"Gail showed it to me this mornin'. Those steers died with the fever, Pony. What else do you know?"

Pony was half sober now. Yet his speech was still thick as he answered. "A fine crew. I rode up the trail a ways with 'em. I never did meet a Texas man who was stingy with the bottle. When I left, they packed a quart away in my saddlebags. I. . . ."

"But what did you find?" Beauregard's temper was wearing thin.

Pony raised his brows. "Plenty. The after-noon they swung north from the Bend City crossin', Bill Fears rode out and paid cash for them critters I spotted comin' across the river. You say the rest are dead?"

This was all Beauregard needed. He didn't even bother to reply to the question. What he said was: "You'd better ride back to the layout and sleep it off, Pony. The rest of us have a job on our hands."

"What kind of a job?" Pony blinked his tired old eyes and shook his head to clear it.

"I'm payin' a call on Bill Fears. The boys are ridin' up there tonight to keep an eye on the layout."

"Then I'll side you."

"Not this time. Better ride home and sober up like I say."

Although no man could have told it, Pony Murdock was sober now. For better than a week, he'd had his fling with an easy-going crew and the alcohol in his guts now was like so much water. Jim Beauregard was headed into trouble, real trouble, and now was no time to back down on him. Yet Pony could tell from the tone of Jim's voice that what he had said was final; he wouldn't have a drunk siding him on what lay ahead. Neither would Pony see Jim ride into the thing alone. So, an inner cunning asserting itself, he readily agreed, even letting his voice go thick as he said: "Suit yourself, Jim. I reckon I can hit that old bunk and sleep around the clock." And with that he raised his hand in a parting gesture and kicked his pony's flanks and rode on down the path left by the trail herd, singing at the top of his lungs.

Beauregard sat there, eying the oldster for a full minute. He was a tolerant man, and even now couldn't blame Pony for his weakness. The old man had supplied him with the one necessary link to Bill Fears's part in what had happened, and he was grateful.

Suddenly impatient to be done with this, Beauregard swung his black east and rode toward the river. And ten minutes later, as dusk settled over the flat prairie, he looked off to the south and made out Pony's fast-disappearing form, now a dot on the dark smear of churned earth that marked the trail herd's passage.

As for Pony, he waited until he could no longer see Beauregard in the settling dusk. Then he turned off to the east, on a line parallel with the one the Texan had taken. He jerked his roan out of its walk into a trot, muttering to himself: "Damned if he leaves me behind."

■ ■ ■ ■

Trail herd crews don't drink while they're working. But Pony, that first night while he sat alongside the fire and talked and drank with those soft-voiced Texans, hadn't thought of that. If he had searched his memory, he might possibly have recognized the man who replaced the empty bottles with full ones. This man, tall and gaunt and with an evil smirk on his thin-lipped face, had signed on with Bill Fears in the early summer at fighting wages. Ten days ago Bill Fears had sent him south to see Ransom, the trail herd boss, and steer the trail herd toward Bend City. His name was Mordue.

That afternoon, Fears had told Mordue: "Ransom's had his pay and I've got what I want. You're to trail along with him for a few days and make sure no one from Bend City finds out I've bought these steers."

What Fears forgot to tell Mordue was that Pony Murdock was now Jim Beauregard's man. If Mordue had known that, he could have climbed into the saddle, ridden out into the night, and put a .30-30 bullet through Pony's spine. As it was, Mordue was only faintly irritated by Pony's presence, and decided that the best way to handle him was to keep him drunk a few days and then forget him. By that time, Bill Fears would have finished with his work.

So Mordue bought a few quarts of the cook's whiskey, and Pony got drunk and stayed that way. When Ransom became suspicious, Mordue explained: "This old jasper's a friend of the sheriff's. If he's missin' for a few days, it'll throw a good scare into Wiley. Maybe it'll pay him back some for not lettin' you ford Bull River."

Ransom readily agreed, since he and Wiley had had bitter, words. This detour was costing Ransom an extra week on the trail, and his temper was ugly as a result.

The cook's supply of whiskey lasted nearly as long as Mordue's money. On the eighth day, Pony decided to turn back.

Before he left, in one of his more sober moments, he sought out Ransom who was riding point, with four other men. He told the rancher: "If you're ever in Bend City, look me up and we'll break open a bottle."

He held out his hand and the rancher took it. Then Pony put the question he'd been wanting for days to ask. "How much was it Fears paid you for them critters, Ransom?" He asked it off-handedly.

"Not enough," Ransom replied, before he thought. Then he tried to cover his slip of the tongue. "What steers?"

But Pony was already riding away, chuckling at the rancher's obvious confusion. Ransom looked for Mordue, but Fears's man had heard that Pony was starting back that day and had fallen far behind the herd to wait until Pony rode past. Mordue wasn't suspicious, but now, with his job finished and in a strange country, he wanted to be sure of the way back to Bend City. He wasn't particularly anxious for Pony's company, either, since the oldster's everlasting tales bored him. So he let Pony get nearly out of sight ahead before he followed.

For the two days they were on the trail, Pony taking a short cut toward Bull River, Mordue kept the oldster well in sight. Each night he made his camp within sight of Pony's fire.

When Pony met Jim Beauregard and talked with him, late on the afternoon of the third day, Mordue was hidden behind a mesquite thicket less than half a mile up the trail. And when Beauregard headed east, toward the Pitchfork, Bill Fears's rider guessed that the old man must know something, after all, and spurred his tired horse to a run, no longer interested in Pony's doings.

It took him two hours to bring the lights

of the Pitchfork into sight, and, when he swung into the corral yard, his horse went down under him from exhaustion.

Bill Fears, in his office, listened to Mordue's story. Then he sat chewing his after supper cigar for the space of a full quarter minute. Finally he looked across at Mordue. "You did a good job. Go on down and get some sleep. Send the boys up here."

He stood on the porch outside his office until he counted fifteen men standing at the foot of the steps. Then he told them briefly what had happened, warning them that Beauregard knew the whole thing and was doubtless headed for the Pitchfork even now.

"And he won't be alone," he told them. "This jasper has plenty between the ears, and he'll have his crew with him when he comes. Split up in pairs and get out there and wait for them. When they come, throw down on 'em, and bring the whole bunch in here. If you can do it without usin' your irons, so much the better."

V

The others hadn't had the time to make the ride from the Olive Branch, so Jim Beauregard swung south after he crossed the river and rode along the east bank. His men would come in this way, along the river, on their way to the hide-out he had mentioned.

He met them three miles to the north of his fence, five riders and two lead broncos packed with blankets and food. They turned the lead horses loose and rode on, straight for the Pitchfork. To the east a quarter moon rose above the far horizon. Beauregard didn't like that, for he would have chosen complete darkness for what lay ahead.

A mile short of the ranch house, he pulled in and waited until his men were grouped alongside.

"We want to make it quick," he told them. "Red and Burley and I will go straight to the house. That leaves three to get down to the bunkhouse and cover it. They may have a guard. If he shoots, keep on goin'. All I care about is taking Fears alive. Don't shoot a man unless you have to, but if you do, see that he goes down to stay. We've got the law on our side, which helps."

He was about to ride on, when a voice sounded harshly from the direction of a stunted cedar, off to his left. "Stay where you are, Beauregard! One of you move, and I'll blow your guts out!"

Jim Beauregard stiffened in his saddle, raising his hands, and looked behind at the

70

others. He saw Red's hand edge toward the rifle in the boot beneath his leg, and cautioned: "Don't, Red."

When he looked ahead again, he could see the two figures that moved out from the cedar's shadow. Each man had a rifle at his shoulder.

One of them whistled, and from far to the right came an answering shout. There was nothing to do but sit there and wait. In less than five minutes three more riders had joined the pair, and from across the bowl-like depression that hid the ranch house and buildings sounded the *thud* of many hoofs.

Twenty minutes later, Beauregard and his men, their holsters and rifle scabbards empty, were herded into the side yard of the house, near the door of Fears's office.

The door opened, and Bill Fears stepped out. He stood there on the porch, looking down at Beauregard with a vicious smile on his heavy face, and said: "This is more like it. Now the rest is easy." He paused, waited for Beauregard to say something. But the Texan only smiled, so Fears went on: "Don't you want to know what I'm going to do with you?"

"Would it help if I did?" Beauregard drawled.

Fears chuckled, gloating over the luck that

had put Beauregard's fate in his hands. "Not much. But I'll tell you anyway. Tomorrow mornin' all six of you will be lying on my side of your fence. The fence will be cut and there'll be two or three hundred head of Pitchfork steers grazin' deep on your range. I'll ride in after the sheriff. He can find his own answer, but, when he does, it'll be plain that the whole bunch of you were cut down while drivin' off one o' my herds. How does that sound?"

"You're forgettin' something," Beauregard drawled. "We saw you drivin' those South Texas steers across the river. The law will want to know about that."

"It's my word against yours, Beauregard. Only you won't be there to give yours."

"It'll be your word against Major Hewes's."

Bill Fears's arrogant smile vanished. "Say that again," he snarled.

"Hewes knows about it, and so does the sheriff," Beauregard said. "It means you're through in this country."

The full meaning of what Beauregard had said made a changed man of Bill Fears. For an instant his arrogance, his proud bearing deserted him. Then he said ominously: "Maybe I'll think up something special for you. . . ."

Suddenly the air rush of a bullet whipped at Fears's feet, and a chip flew from the planking within two inches of his right boot. Immediately, from the slope above the house, shuttled down the brittle explosion of a rifle shot.

An instant later a faraway voice shouted down: "Fears, this is Sheriff Wiley! I've got Major Hewes and a dozen men up here! Drop your guns and turn Beauregard loose or we cut you down!"

Bill Fears stood there, his squat shape turned rigid for the space of two seconds as he realized that he made a perfect target. Then, with the quickness of a cat, he jumped down off the porch, threw himself down behind Beauregard's horse, his words reaching his men, sharp and fast, as he moved: "Get this bunch down to the bunkhouse! I'll take care of Beauregard. If you see a man out there, shoot him!" He had palmed the gun out of the holster on his right thigh, and now reached up and jammed it into Beauregard's ribs, snarling: "Climb down. And be careful, partner."

The thing had happened so quickly that the next shot from far out into the night whipped harmlessly over their heads and struck the side of the house with a loud slap. Fears had judged this nicely, knowing what would happen. So long as Beauregard and his men were here, the sheriff and whoever else was with him would not dare throw any bullets into that knot of horsemen grouped around the porch.

For the next quarter minute, panic gripped these men. Fears barked out his orders time and again, steadying his riders, and finally he and Beauregard and a Pitchfork rider were alone in the lighted office, the rest — the Pitchfork crew and their Olive Branch captives — headed for the bunkhouse.

Fears stood in front of his desk, listening. In another half minute a shot sounded behind the house. It was the signal he had been waiting for. His men were safely in the bunkhouse. He glanced back over his shoulder; Beauregard was sitting in a chair along the back wall, facing the six-gun of the Pitchfork rider. Fears smiled his satisfaction, turned to the desk, and lowered the wicks on the lamp, then walked over to throw open the door.

He stood to one side of the door and shouted: "Wiley, this is Bill Fears talking! I've got Beauregard and I'm keepin' him! If you throw shots this way, we'll put a bullet through his head!"

He waited. After a ten-second interval,

Wiley's voice shuttled down off the slope: "What is it you want, Fears?"

Fears debated his answer. From what little Beauregard had told him, he was wise enough to see that he had lost. He was through in this country and would be lucky to get out alive. His wild hopes of someday seeing all this range under his brand had gone up in smoke these last few minutes. There was but one thing left for him — to work out his revenge on the man who had ruined him. So now he called out to the sheriff: "I want two days for me and my men to ride clear of the country! I'll take Beauregard with me!"

A long silence met his words. Then Wiley's voice came again: "I'll come down and talk it over!"

"No talk! This is final! Take it or leave it!"

This time a long, ominous interval followed. Once Fears looked back at Beauregard and said: "If my luck runs bad, yours does, too, friend." There was a meaning behind his words that was plain.

Wiley shouted down once more: "What will you do with Beauregard?"

"Turn him loose when we're clear!"

"You give your word on that?"

"I'll swear it!" was Fears's quick answer.

"Then round up your bunch and start

ridin'! If you break your word, Fears, I'll hunt you down myself!"

Fears wasn't taking any chances. He had Jim Beauregard's wrists bound by a length of rawhide. Then, making Beauregard walk in front of him, he stepped out of his office and onto the porch and called his crew from the bunkhouse.

Under the threat of the guns lined at them out of the darkness, Fears and his riders mounted their ponies and started out of the yard. Beauregard rode his black gelding alongside Fears, and had his last look at his five men, standing in front of the bunk-house.

Red called out: "Say the word and we'll get our guns and drag along behind, Jim!"

"That'd be a sure way of losin' your boss, cowpoke," Fears jeered.

They were gone then, and, when the darkness swallowed the last disappearing rider, Sheriff Wiley and Major Hewes rode into the yard and up to the group of Texans. Red was swearing violently, calling for someone to go to Fears's office and get their guns.

Wiley cut in on his string of oaths. "Take it easy, Red. This is once we'll have to trust Bill Fears. Jim will be back."

Red snorted in disgust and helplessness. "We'll never see him again," was his ominous prediction.

Pony Murdock's luck was holding. A few minutes before, a Pitchfork rider had come within twenty feet of the spot where Pony sat his tired roan, leaning forward in the saddle with one hand clamped about the animal's nostrils. The roan had lifted one hoof and brought it down solidly with a noise sounding as loudly as the crack of a gun. But a split second later there was a commotion farther along the slope as Beauregard and his men were surprised, and the rider had gone on to see what was happening.

After that, Pony tied the roan to a low-growing bush and walked closer in to the house. When he saw that Jim and the rest were being led in, unarmed, he started to work his way around to the front of the house. His two cap-and-ball pistols were in his gnarled fists. He wasn't sure what he could do against that crew, but at least he'd make a try.

Then came the shots from up the hill, the parley with the sheriff, and Pony had to stand up there and watch Beauregard ride away, a prisoner.

As the knot of horsemen below disappeared into the night, Pony had an idea that sent him running back for the roan. In the saddle once more, he swung wide of the layout and set out after the Pitchfork crew. But the roan was tired, and Pony, needing a bracer, was less careful and cautious than he should have been.

They heard him coming. Fears turned in his saddle, raised his short-barreled .45, and called: "Stay where you are!"

Pony was surprised. He wasn't expecting to overtake them so soon. In his panic, he streaked up one of his guns, lined it at a man he vaguely recognized as Bill Fears, and pulled the trigger.

That shot sent Bill Fears's black Stetson whirling from his head to the ground. The bullet had grazed Fears's scalp. His one thought was that Wiley and his posse had circled and had laid an ambush along the trail.

Stark fear rode through the man for the first time in his life. Blended with it was an impotent fury that made him turn in his saddle and jerk his weapon around at Jim Beauregard, riding alongside. He was an instant too late. Beauregard, not knowing the meaning of the shot, had seen Fears turn his back. As the man had moved, Beauregard raised his bound hands and kneed the black close in to the other's horse.

Abruptly Fears whirled about, and Beauregard's two fists slashed down in a hard blow, knocking the swinging gun down as it exploded.

Jim felt the sting of a powder burn along his thigh. All at once the black stumbled and fell with a bullet through his back. Jim rolled clear, seeing Fears fall from his saddle at the force of his blow.

Fighting wages — $100 a month and found, as Fears paid it — will buy a man's guns but not his loyalty. The Pitchfork crew would face any number in the open. But now, as the second shot crashed out of the blackness behind, Fears's hardcases scattered, expecting each instant to see the blaze of powder flashes wink out of the surrounding darkness.

Jim Beauregard came to his knees in time to see Fears make a wild lunge after his bucking horse and miss catching a hold on the reins. Then Fears was on his feet, swinging his .45 in an upward arc as Beauregard left the ground in a rolling dive. The gun exploded as Jim's weight crashed against Bill Fears's thighs. Beauregard felt the bullet take him high in his right shoulder, yet he felt no pain until his weight thudded heavily on Fears's outstretched bulk.

His wrists tied, all Jim could do was bring

his fists slashing down at Bill Fears's gun hand. He beat the gun aside, but now Fears, held down by Beauregard's weight, swung the weapon in a vicious, clubbing blow. Time and again he struck at Jim's head, never getting in a solid blow. Jim brought up his arms to shield his face, and instantly felt Fears's weight roll from under him.

Fears surged to his feet and was almost erect when the spur on his left boot caught in the cuff of Jim's Levi's and threw him off balance. In that half-second interval, Jim Beauregard straightened from his crouch and rammed his two fists into the rancher's face. As Fears fell backward, blood streaming from his cut lips, Jim reached out and tore the second weapon from the holster on the Pitchfork owner's thigh.

Fears sat down awkwardly, his right arm free and swinging up the six-gun. Jim whipped the heavy Colt's into line and thumbed back the hammer and let it fall. Timed to the solid whip of the weapon in his hand, he saw Fears's wide bulk jerk with the impact of the lead slug as it took him in the chest.

But some superhuman strength gave Bill Fears the power to steady his .45 and pull the trigger. The force of the bullet, smashing against his ribs on his left side, spun Jim

Beauregard halfway around. Then, as the pain of the wound sent him almost into unconsciousness, he lined his weapon once again and emptied it at Fears in a staccato gun thunder ended finally by the *click* of the hammer on an empty cartridge.

When the others — Wiley, Major Hewes, and Beauregard's men — rode to the spot a minute later, Pony Murdock was kneeling alongside Jim's sprawled form, muttering in a choked voice a choice selection from his lengthy vocabulary of profanity.

The major swung down and pushed Pony aside. He tore away Beauregard's shirt and inspected the chest wound first, the one in the shoulder next. Then he glanced up at Pony, who was still swearing, and said reassuringly: "All he needs is some water and a few bandages."

Major Hewes was wrong. Jim Beauregard was moved to the Pitchfork ranch house that night and it was four days before he opened his eyes. By that time his lung wound had closed and the broken bones in his shoulder had begun to mend.

Gail Hewes was sitting in a chair alongside the bed when Jim moved his head and looked at her. For a moment she sat there in wide-eyed incredulity. Then, realizing that he was not only alive but looking at her with his gray eyes betraying something she longed to see in them, she choked back a sob and leaned down and kissed him.

Later that day, when the doctor was sure that the worst was over, Pony Murdock stepped into Beauregard's room. Gail, seeing the flush of embarrassment that reddened the oldster's face, went out the door and closed it behind her.

"They tell me you started that scrap, Pony," said Jim.

"I reckon I did," the oldster admitted. "Just like the first one. I stopped in to say so long."

"Leavin'?" Beauregard asked. "Why?"

"I might mess up somethin' else for you."

Jim Beauregard laughed, with a ring in his voice that sounded good to Pony. "If it hadn't been for you, I wouldn't be alive, Pony. Fears wouldn't have turned me loose."

"You mean that, Jim?" Pony's old voice was proud and joyful.

Jim nodded. "And another thing. In a month or so I'll be needin' a best man. You're it."

Wanted for Blackmail

"Wanted for Blackmail" was completed early in December, 1936. It was submitted by Jon Glidden's agent to Popular Publications and was bought on April 8, 1937. It appeared under the title "Tin Star Town-Tamer" in *10 Story Western* (5/37). The author was paid $81.00. For its appearance here the author's title and full text have been restored.

I

Seeing the way Mike O'Hara's square, loose figure so completely filled the chair by the window, Sheriff Walt Crowe grudgingly admitted that it would take quite a man to cross the big Irishman and make it stick. Thinking this, he toned down his words.

"I've got proof, Mike."

"You're wrong," O'Hara stated emphatically. As though the matter was settled, he shifted his gaze from the lawman's thin, mustached face, moved his feet a little closer to the stove, and looked out of the jail office window again.

For ten years Walt Crowe had used patience in his dealings with Mike O'Hara. He used it now in not speaking. Pushing his swivel chair back from the desk, he opened a drawer. He shoved back the nearly full pint bottle of whiskey that lay atop the litter of papers. After rummaging a moment, he found what he wanted and shut the drawer. He straightened up and tossed a crisp, new Reward notice onto the far side of the desk, near O'Hara.

"Read it, Mike."

O'Hara turned from the window and, with obvious effort, brought his attention back to the matter at hand. He gave Crowe a long look before he thrust out a fat hand to pick up the paper and read what was written below the dim photograph in the center:

WANTED FOR MURDER
REWARD
$3,000
FOUR FINGER CUMMINGS:
Height 5' 7", hair blond, eyes gray,
weight 155 lbs., index finger missing
from right hand. On Feb. 17, 1884,
shot and killed Roy Thurston,

Marshal of Flat Butte, Wyo. Participated in stage robbery at Sundance, Wyo., late in same year. Aliases Frank Camden, Idaho Cummings, Hal Caden. Address information to U.S. Marshal W.L. Trent, Flat Butte, Wyo. DEAD OR ALIVE: Dangerous if armed.

O'Hara took a long time to read the notice, yet Crowe, knowing the man, was undisturbed. At length Mike's eyes raised from the sheet to regard the sheriff.

"That checks, don't it?" Crowe asked.

O'Hara sighed and bent forward in the chair. Without answering, he tore the paper in two, crumpled the two pieces, and laid them on the desk. Next, he struck a match and touched the flame to the paper.

"Just a minute now, Mike. . . ."

O'Hara's upraised hand cut short the lawman's words. The big Irishman sat out the silence until the Reward notice had burned to a gray ash, then smiled and said quietly: "Forget you ever saw this, Walt."

Anger, sudden and unreasoning, loosed itself within Crowe. He realized then, for the first time since he had known the man, that he hated O'Hara. For years he had taken luck as it ran, uncomplaining when he had to swallow his pride. O'Hara could ask him to do this; he had, in a way, a right to do it.

"That needs explainin', Mike," he drawled.

"Since when do I owe you any explanations, Crowe?"

The sheriff's face took on a slight flush, although his expression remained inscrutable. He was hating himself, asking why it was that he could never make the break that would, once and for all, end Mike O'Hara's domination over him. He felt a flash of his old confidence, and in that moment he knew he could kill O'Hara — that he was more than a match for the Irishman when it came to guns. But some cautious streak within him gave warning that this was not the time.

"I can't let you get away with everything, Mike," he said levelly. "Is there any good reason why I shouldn't go over to your place and arrest that gun-slick killer?"

"I hired him last night."

For the space of five long seconds Walt Crowe searched his mind to find the reason behind this move of O'Hara's. He gave it up finally.

"Three thousand is a lot, and I'm a poor

man," he said. Then again: "It's no good letting a hardcase like Caden run loose in Mound City."

O'Hara straightened the string tie along his immaculate white shirt front, regarding the law man with an unwinking stare. At length he said pointedly: "Seems like I remember another Reward notice. Could you be wantin' me to tack that up over in my place, Walt?"

Here it was. It was no surprise, even though Mike O'Hara had never mentioned it. Ten years ago it had been that old Reward notice that had enabled O'Hara to recognize Crowe by another name — a man who had wearied of the law's pursuit. O'Hara had seen his chance and taken it; from then on, Walt Crowe was protected by the law, hiding behind a badge in O'Hara's town. By enforcing the law O'Hara's way, he had bought silence.

Now, once again, Mike was using the club he held over his lawman. Crowe asked himself just how this case differed from the dozen others that should have put O'Hara outside the law, deciding at length that it didn't. So it was that he gave his answer: "Since you put it that way, Mike, I never heard of Caden."

It went against everything in Crowe's

make-up to force out those words. They took something from him, cheapened him in his own eyes. A subtle change rode through him, and gradually he felt the gnawing hunger for liquor — the hunger that had been with him constantly for months. He reached down and took the bottle out of the drawer. Lifting out the cork, he extended it to Mike O'Hara.

"Have a drink?"

O'Hara's wide lips came down in a half sneer. Disgust mirrored itself on his pink, round face.

"Not now," he answered, and watched while Crowe tilted the bottle to his lips and took a long pull. He added, when the other was through: "Don't get any haywire ideas, Walt."

The sheriff's gray eyes hardened a trifle. When he spoke, his words were spaced evenly: "I wouldn't rub it in if I were you, Mike."

Pushing himself up out of the chair, O'Hara went to the door. There he hesitated, looking up the street.

Crowe got up and threw two rounds of wood into the stove, and then went to the window. The expression on his face was one of weariness now that the other was not looking. His gaze followed O'Hara's. Up the deeply rutted street, coming toward them, was a buckboard flanked by two riders. The driver, a girl, wheeled in toward the hitch rack a few doors above the jail with the skilful abandon of one long familiar with the handling of the team.

A light of admiration crept into the sheriff's eyes as he watched the girl climb down from the seat and go to the rail to tie the team. She wore a split buckskin skirt and a heavy wool jacket. In the shadow beneath the wide-brimmed hat, her regular features took on an olive shade, and Crowe decided that he had never seen a finer face.

The two riders who had come in with the buckboard waved a casual farewell to her. They rode on past the jail and turned in at the hitch rack in front of the saloon across the street. The Golden Eagle was O'Hara's place, the most prosperous of the three the town boasted.

It was the rider half a head taller than the other who took Crowe's attention. He wore the faded blue denim trousers of the range, a dusty jacket against the chill of the winter day, and broad-brimmed, gray Stetson. Crowe noticed the economy of motion he used in getting out of the saddle and in rail-haltering his sorrel. As he crossed the walk, he moved with a confident, swinging stride.

As soon as the two had disappeared through the swing doors, the sheriff spoke aloud to O'Hara, who still stood in the door at his side.

"Looks like Stony Enders is what the Triangle R needed, don't it, Mike?"

Something in those words caused Mike O'Hara to turn slowly to face him. There was a look in his gray eyes that telegraphed a warning to Crowe.

"Just what the hell do you mean by that, Tin Star?"

A quick understanding came to the sheriff. The knowledge of it braced him.

"Just what I said, Mike. With Stony out there helpin' Jo and Ralph, it looks like they'd be able to pay you off that loan this spring."

With an expression grown out of twenty years at handling cards, O'Hara shrugged, masking his feelings once more. "I'd rather have the money than the spread," was all he said.

Whatever the danger had been, Crowe sensed that it had passed. He even wondered whether his first guess had been the right one. He could feel the whiskey taking hold of him now, and it gave him confidence. "Sometimes," he said, "I figure it was a good thing when old Hap Redburn cashed in his chips and gave those two kids a chance to put the layout on its feet again. Whiskey and ranchin' don't mix, beyond a certain point, which is somethin' Hap could never figure out."

Purposely he was not looking at O'Hara as he spoke. If he had been, he would have caught the hard expression returning to the saloon owner's eyes. Here was something Crowe had been wanting to talk over with O'Hara for a long time, in fact, for eight months — ever since Hap Redburn's death and the discovery of the Triangle R's indebtedness.

The whiskey had mellowed Crowe, and he rambled on, paying no thought to the consequences: "It's a cinch young Ralph Redburn couldn't have managed it alone. He's different from his sister. If it weren't for Enders, they'd be losin' the outfit this spring."

He heard O'Hara's step beside him, but turned too late. The Irishman's ham-like fist gathered in Crowe's shirt front and twisted it. Two of the buttons came off and fell onto the floor. Mike's face was close and his eyes were slitted.

"Get this, Crowe," he growled hoarsely. "You aren't bein' paid to think. I don't want the Triangle R . . . never have wanted it."

He shoved the lawman back against the desk, loosed his grip, and turned suddenly back toward the door. There he paused, adding: "So long as your sentiments don't override your good judgment, I don't give one damn what you think. You know how far you can go without steppin' on my toes, Crowe." He paused a moment, letting his words carry their full weight. "Only don't forget . . . I can build a noose for you any time I choose."

Then O'Hara was gone. Crowe's gaze, flint-like, followed his progress across the street and into the Golden Eagle. For the first time in his life he had let a man live after laying hands on him.

He found himself cursing savagely, uttering words that had not passed his lips for years. But gradually, and with a persistence that would not be denied, the things O'Hara had said about the Triangle R crowded his resentment into the background and left him with a growing curiosity.

Here was something he could not ignore. Thinking over the words that had brought that outburst from O'Hara, he remembered suddenly that day, eight months ago, that had seen him standing beside the bed of his dying friend, Hap Redburn. A hushed silence had hung over the room. Once again, Redburn's words came back, startlingly clear: *Walt, you're the only one I can leave Jo and Ralph with. Look after them for me. See if you can find Ralph and bring him home. It's a damned shame Jo isn't a man, or she wouldn't need his help.*

Two hours later Redburn was dead. It took three weeks for an advertisement of his father's death in a northern Montana paper to reach Ralph Redburn and bring him home. He brought with him Stony Enders, and it was Enders who had since supplied the driving energy that had lifted the Triangle R out from under Hap Redburn's legacy of debt. Fences were patched, water holes cleaned, and it was Enders himself who had warned off the thieving nesters and made the order stick.

And now, certain that he was seeing Jo and Ralph Redburn building a solid foundation for the future, Walt Crowe found that Mike O'Hara planned on owning the outfit. There was nothing beyond Mike's resentment to furnish him proof, yet it was obvious. It had been a bad day when Hap Redburn, his loan refused at the bank, had gone to Mike O'Hara and borrowed the money he needed. Already O'Hara owned three small ranches he had acquired in exactly this manner. The Triangle R would have made a rich prize for O'Hara's $5,000 investment.

Then Crowe remembered that less than a week ago Ralph Redburn had stopped in at the office. He had purposely mentioned the note to Crowe, telling him that the money would be in the bank in another thirty days.

"Then we can use the paper to light fires with, Walt," he had said.

Apparently there was nothing that could keep Jo and Ralph from meeting their obligation. Reassured, Crowe resumed his seat at the desk, thinking that now the time had come when he would have to do something about O'Hara. The old feeling of despondency returned; once again his hand dipped down to the drawer to bring out the bottle.

It took him half an hour to empty it. Five minutes later he hailed a boy passing the office, and sent him across to the Golden Eagle after a quart of Old Crow.

The afternoon dragged. Feeling the pleasant glow of the liquor, he forgot his troubles and began to think that, after all, he could have worse luck than working for Mike O'Hara. He dozed and did not wake until after sundown. The fire in the stove had gone out. He was cold and hungry.

Going down the street toward the lunchroom, he saw Enders and Redburn come out of the Golden Eagle. Ralph swayed drunkenly as he came across the walk, and Stony Enders had to help him into the saddle.

Like his old man, Walt mused, allowing himself a silent chuckle. *The boys have been celebratin'.*

He watched the two until they had ridden into the night's thick shadows up the street, then went on his way to his supper.

II

Into the chill dawn of the next morning rode Walt Crowe, the liquor of the night before setting up in him a half-nauseous, half-throbbing discomfort. Four o'clock was too early an hour to get even so much as a cup of coffee — but for that, he would not have minded this early ride.

Thinking of Flint McNeil's ugly face, he silently cursed the man. It was Flint, a Triangle R rider, who had telephoned half an hour ago that a Triangle R line shack had been burned during the night. Would Crowe come out right away and help them cut for sign and hunt the men who had done it?

Crowe had been too sleepy to catch the full meaning of the thing. The telephone was new to him, and he seldom wasted more words than necessary in using it. But now that he was awake once again, he regretted that he had not asked McNeil for more particulars.

Was Mike O'Hara taking this obvious way of striking at the Triangle R? Or had the nesters rebelled over being cut off so suddenly from the bounty that had been theirs during Hap Redburn's lifetime? Crowe shook his head, deciding that O'Hara would use no such tactics as this. Wholesale rustling would be more in O'Hara's line if he chose to ruin the outfit.

He gave up trying to find the answer to his questions and wrapped his leather coat tighter about him to shut out the penetrating chill. The trail ran, table-flat, over rock and sand, with here and there the patches of bunch grass that made it possible to work the range. Occasional rock outcroppings thrust up out of the thin soil, taking on grotesque outlines in the half light from the graying horizon ahead.

Six miles beyond town the trail made a wide swing around a massive outcropping that angled skyward toward the dimming stars. It was here that Crowe saw the thing that brought him suddenly alert. Against the lighter shadows of the uptilted rock showed the outline of two saddled horses. Even before he was close enough to distinguish their brands, he recognized the thick-chested sorrel Stony Enders had ridden into town the day before.

The discovery turned him instantly wary. He rode a quick circle around the outcropping, bending low over his saddle so as to form a smaller target for the danger he was certain lurked there. But soon he straightened, seeing the two huddled figures lying at the base of a thick point of rock that thrust up skyward. The light was strong enough now so that he could pick out the details. Stony Enders lay on his back, with arms spread-eagled while one outstretched hand was loosely closed over the butt of a .45. Crowe took all this in, then edged in closer to see the thing that sent his blood running cold.

The inhumanly sprawled position of Ralph Redburn's thin frame told him the man was dead. Even before he drew rein close enough to see the dark bloodstain across the back of the canvas coat, between the shoulders, he knew it.

The ring of his chestnut's hoof on rock seemed to telegraph a warning to Stony Enders, for at that moment he stirred. Crowe sat his saddle, watching, his six-gun out now, while Enders rolled over and pushed himself up to a sitting position with obvious difficulty. He leaned forward, with his head pillowed in his hands as though in pain. At length he looked up, recognized the lawman, and glanced about him with a bewildered expression crossing his set features.

He stared at Crowe and asked in a thin voice: "How come?"

Walt Crowe shook his head, but made no answer, noting that Enders paid no attention to the weapon that had fallen from his hand when he sat up.

Stony looked over at Ralph. His lips twisted in an attempt at a smile. "If I could move, I'd crawl over and wake Ralph. But my head's splittin'. What happened, Sheriff?"

"Take another look at Ralph," Crowe answered evenly, dismounting.

Enders looked again, and what he saw made him come hastily to his feet. He staggered over to look down at his friend. All at once he went down on his knees beside Ralph and gently rolled him over. A choked cry broke from his lips. He looked up at Crowe, a bitter grief written across features gone suddenly ashen.

"He's dead!"

Crowe stood watching until Stony was on his feet again.

"What do you know about this?" Stony asked, his voice brittle with emotion. "Who killed him?"

The lawman nodded toward the Colt that lay on the ground where Enders had dropped it. Stony walked over to it, moving a little unsteadily. His hand dropped to feel of his empty holster, and Crowe caught the quick flicker of astonishment that dilated his eyes.

When Enders spoke, his voice was hushed: "Did I do it?"

Walt Crowe made his decision quickly, knowing he could not be wrong.

"No," he answered, shaking his head. "But I reckon the man who did wanted me to think it was you."

Stony sat down again, holding his head with both hands. "I didn't drink enough last night to make me feel this way."

The sheriff's face was seamed in a deep frown. "Maybe you ought to tell me what happened."

Stony's eyes came suddenly alight. "It was the last drink Mike gave us. That was it, Walt!" He was on his feet again, standing close to the lawman, a subtle fury turning his dark face into an ugly grimace. "I knew it tasted damned funny. And Mike said it was his own private bottle . . . one on the house. Hell, Walt, I didn't have more'n five drinks . . . just enough to go along with Ralph and keep him company while he got a skin full."

Walt nodded. "Ralph was drunk?"

"Just like he always was when he hit the bottle," Stony told him. "I've kept him away from it for weeks now. But yesterday we were celebratin'. . . ." He paused, left the sentence unfinished.

"Celebratin' what?"

"It was nothin'," Stony said, his glance shifting. "Ralph figured we ought to have a few drinks, though, seein' that Jo and I are goin' to be married soon."

So that was it. Walt Crowe could even now feel a little proud of Jo Redburn and the choice she had made. He had liked Enders from the very moment he had met him. Once it had occurred to him that the man would make a fine husband for Jo, but he had been so out of touch with things at the Triangle R that he had little realization of what had been going on out there.

He heard himself saying: "She's a fine girl, Stony. This is goin' to be hard on her." His thoughts were a jumble, yet he gradually caught the implication Ralph Redburn's death would leave. He voiced the thought: "With Ralph out of the way and you marryin' Jo, it looks like you've got yourself a ranch, Stony."

He put the statement bluntly, and waited to see the results. They were not long in coming. A look of disbelief crossed Stony Enders's face, to be followed by one of incredible fury. All at once Stony lunged!

Had it not been for Stony's stiffened muscles, Walt Crowe could not have evaded the blow. As it was, it caught him on the shoulder, throwing him back a step. Enders fell against him and would have gone down if Crowe had not reached out to take him roughly by the arm.

Stony straightened up, jerking his arm away. He flashed a glance back to where his gun lay in the sand — and took a step toward it.

Crowe stopped him. "Easy, Stony. No sense in goin' hog-wild. I'm just tellin' you what people will think. I know different."

Enders gave the lawman a steady glance. At length he mumbled: "For a minute I wondered about you, Walt." He rubbed his palm along his forehead, closing his eyes in pain.

"What about that drink Mike O'Hara gave you last night?" Crowe asked, knowing the torture that Enders was experiencing. "Did it taste bitter?"

"Bitter as gall."

"Why did you drink it?"

"Ralph had just told Mike he'd be able to pay off the note. Mike was settin' us up. I had to take it."

"Ralph, too?"

Stony nodded. "It finished Ralph. A half mile out o' town he folded up. I had to lay him across the saddle. Things aren't very clear after that. I remember ridin', tryin' to sit up straight. That's all."

Crowe walked over to pick up Stony's .45. He sniffed at the blunt snout of the weapon, then threw open the loading gate, and shucked out the shells. He held out his hand and showed Stony. There were two empties.

"That tallies," he said. "Ralph was shot only once. You carry an empty under the hammer?"

Stony nodded. "But, Walt. I don't remember. . . ."

"I know you don't," Crowe answered. "It takes a real man to handle knockout drops and still hang onto his senses. Did you pour your own drink?"

"No. O'Hara took the bottle out of a cupboard behind the bar and poured them himself."

The sheriff snorted his disgust. "I'd think you'd know better."

Enders had no comment to make. He stood there, staring blankly at Ralph's still form with a look that brought Walt Crowe abruptly out of his ill humor.

"You're goin' to jail, Stony."

"Jail?" Enders was slow to comprehend. "But I didn't do it, Walt! Give me my iron and I'll hunt the whippoorwill who did!"

Crowe shook his head soberly, repeating: "You're goin' to jail. Whoever did this, figured I'd take you there. Flint McNeil called in this mornin' to tell me your line shack up Three Way Gulch burned last night. I was meant to ride out here and find you."

"Then I've been framed?"

"Good and proper."

There was a glitter in Stony's eyes as he looked over once more at Ralph's body. Crowe knew what was going on in the man's mind.

"It won't do to make a break for Ralph's six-gun," he said. "You could grab it and throw down on me and maybe get away. But that wouldn't help any. What'd happen to Jo?"

The words had their effect. Enders's

shoulders drooped, all the life going out of him.

"You see?" Crowe went on. "Someone wanted mighty bad to have you and Ralph out of the way. If you run, the law will be after you. You'd better stay and wait till things clear up a bit."

"How can they, with me in jail?"

"Your guess is as good as mine. But it looks to me like Mike O'Hara would bear watchin'. Did you see this man Caden last night?"

"Caden?" Stony shook his head. "Who's he?"

"Little fellow with yellow hair. He carries his guns tied low."

"Oh, him." Stony's look changed to one of understanding. "He was around most of the afternoon. Sat in at a poker game and left half an hour or so before we did. I saw him go out."

Crowe mused: "It couldn't have been anyone else." For a moment he was silent, then added: "You pack Ralph into his saddle. I'm havin' a look around."

It took him five minutes to go over the ground around the outcropping. When he came back, Stony had slung Ralph's body across the saddle and tied it so that it would not slip off.

"There's no sign," Crowe said. "Let's ride."

The ride back to Mound City was a silent one. The red ball of the sun thrust up over the horizon, throwing quarter-mile shadows out ahead of them along the trail. A mile out of town Crowe reined in beside Enders. He brought out a pair of handcuffs from a back pocket.

"You'd better wear these. It'll look a little more convincin'."

Stony gave him a look of distrust. "What's to stop you from carryin' out Mike O'Hara's play, Crowe? You're his man."

III

The bluntly accusing words hit the sheriff between the eyes. He held back the stinging reply that first came to his lips, knowing that Stony Enders could have no reason for trust in him. To Stony he was nothing but a lawman who spent most of his time over a bottle.

He replied simply. "I was Hap Redburn's best friend, Enders."

Stony hesitated, and Crowe wondered what was going on in his mind. At last Enders said: "Ralph trusted you, and so does Jo. I reckon I spoke out of turn, Walt." He held out his hands.

Ten minutes later the two rode into town, directly to the jail. The half dozen people they passed on the street spread the news quickly, and, by the time Enders was locked into one of the four cells, a crowd gathered in front.

Crowe took Ralph's body down to the hardware store, where Ed Kennedy put it in his back storeroom to await burial. Next he went to the hotel, and put through a call to the Triangle R. It was a party line, and he knew there would be listeners. So he did not ask to speak to Jo, but gave his message to Flint McNeil, who had been waiting for him at the house.

That disagreeable task completed, he walked quickly down to the jail, dispersed the curious crowd that had gathered, and sent a boy over to the restaurant for two breakfasts. The office was cold, so he built a fire in the stove.

Stony was not hungry, but Crowe forced him to eat.

"You'll need all the food you can cram in you," the sheriff said. "And sleep, too. Now leave everything to me. Don't let anything you hear outside get you riled up. It'll be night before anyone tries to get in here. And, by then, I hope you'll be out."

Stony was not slow to comprehend the

meaning behind the sheriff's words. "You mean . . . you mean there'll be a mob?"

Crowe nodded. "I'd bet money on it. But nothin' can happen until after dark. The word's already spreadin' to gather up a necktie party."

What he said was true. He had heard of it at the hotel, and only then was he sure he was progressing along the right lines. No man but Mike O'Hara would have started that kind of talk with so little to back it up. Crowe himself had told no one any details of Enders's arrest. Ed Kennedy, at the hardware store, could be depended on to keep what he knew to himself.

Stony took in the lawman's words as though he had half expected them. After a minute he asked: "Does Jo know?"

"I called up and told Flint McNeil. She'll be in this afternoon."

He went out of the cell-block then, took down the double-barreled shotgun from the wall, and broke it open. He loaded the gun, and laid it across his desk.

By noontime the single street of Mound City was alive with buckboards, spring wagons, and horses. The Golden Eagle was doing a thriving business. Crowe could see three of O'Hara's men — Wade Sanderson, Al Hardy, and Ben Nilsen — mixing unobtrusively with those who came and went, picking their men and pausing to talk with them. It was obvious to the sheriff that they were stirring up the crowd with lynch talk. Yet he was certain he could not be wrong — it would not happen until night.

Several times Crowe felt a gnawing hunger for liquor, but each time he put it down. He knew that he would need a clear head.

Shortly after two o'clock, Crowe spotted Fred Benson, owner of the Skillet outfit, coming down the street. Of all the people Walt Crowe knew around Mound City, this man was the one he could trust beyond question. Crowe had been hoping Benson would show up.

Benson stopped just outside the door, saying: "There's talk of a lynchin', Walt. Al Hardy, across the street, tells it that you found Enders out by Six Mile Rocks. Redburn had a hole through his back . . . and Enders's Forty-Five had been fired."

"Uhn-huh," Crowe drawled. "And where did Hardy get all this?"

"He didn't say."

"Fred, I haven't told a soul where or how I found Enders and Ralph Redburn. We didn't meet anyone on the trail . . . and no one saw us. Figure it out for yourself."

Fred Benson's face underwent a slow

change. When he spoke, the tone of his voice was a little lower than usual and he put his words deliberately: "I never knew you to lie, Crowe. Who framed him?"

The sheriff shook his head. "I'm keepin' my guesses to myself."

"Enders won't live to come to trial. A lot of folks are talkin' up rope and limb trial tonight. You'd better get busy."

"I aim to . . . with your help."

Benson answered: "I'm in on it. What can I do?"

Crowe handed the shotgun to him. "Don't let anyone in here while I'm gone. It'll take me about half an hour to do what I want."

"Mind tellin' me what it is?"

"Don't know yet," Crowe said hurriedly. "After I get back, I want you to get three or four of your men and throw around this jail without anyone knowin' it. Tell 'em to stay under cover, but to keep their eyes open. I don't think they'll be needed, but I'm not takin' chances."

As he finished, he pulled open the desk drawer and lifted out the bottle he had left there the night before. He took a swallow of the whiskey without offering any to Benson, then poured a little in his palm and smeared it on his shirt.

Benson, incredulous, watched him. "What

the hell is this, Walt?"

"I'm stagin' a drunk," Crowe told him, and went out the front door and onto the street. Behind him trailed the aroma of whiskey.

Crossing the street, Walt Crowe weaved a little in his spraddled stride. He wore no coat, but nevertheless walked loosely even though the chill air made him shiver. He edged through the crowd at the door of the Golden Eagle, looking with a flat, vacant stare at those who spoke to him. Once through the swing doors, he went directly to the bar, noting that the men in the room made way for him. At the bar he ordered a double shot of whiskey with a small beer chaser.

Lifting the brimming glass to his lips, he spilled a little onto his leather cuff, but made no move to wipe it off. Nodding to the door at the end of the bar, he said to the bartender: "Mike in?"

"Busy."

He paid no attention to the barkeep's reply. He shoved the man standing alongside him out of his way, and walked uncertainly to the door of Mike O'Hara's office. He did not knock before opening the door.

Hal Caden came out of his chair in front of O'Hara's desk, and his hand dropped to the six-gun at his thigh. O'Hara held out his hand to stop him, looking with undisguised displeasure at the sheriff.

"I'm after orders, Mike."

He closed the door behind him. Now the noise from the barroom was shut out, leaving a tense, strained silence.

O'Hara's thick brows contracted in a frown. At a nod from him, Caden gave the sheriff a last cursory glance and left the room. Crowe sat down.

"Orders?" Mike queried.

"Enders is locked up. What am I to do with him?" Crowe's words were slurred, and he winked significantly.

O'Hara said: "Been hittin' the bottle again, Walt? You're drunk."

Crowe straightened up with a show of indignation. "Drunk? Gawdamighty, Mike, can't a man have a drink or two without bein' drunk? I ain't never been drunk, 'specially with a pris'ner to guard." He paused a moment to lean forward over the desk, then whispered: "Am I to stay out o' the way, Mike?"

"You get over across the street and keep a guard on that jail," O'Hara growled. Then a slow smile crossed his coarse features. "If the crowd gets rough tonight," he drawled, "don't throw any lead into it, Walt. You might hurt a few of the boys."

Crowe screwed his face up into another obvious wink, nodded knowingly, and got up out of the chair. "Mind if I take one on the way out?"

"Help yourself," Mike answered, relaxing, affable once more.

The sheriff went through the door and closed it behind him. It was a full minute before Hal Caden reëntered. When he had come in and closed the door, he caught the pleased smile on Mike O'Hara's face.

"Any news?" he asked.

O'Hara chuckled. "Forget the sheriff, Caden. He's with us."

Outside, at the bar, Walt Crowe lingered for a good twenty minutes. During that time he downed six drinks of straight whiskey. O'Hara's man behind the bar exchanged several knowing smiles with his customers and shook his head solemnly as Crowe left, weaving slightly and staring ahead with unseeing eyes.

IV

Jo Redburn came to the jail shortly after Fred Benson had left to round up his riders. Her eyes were moist with tears. Crowe knew that she had just come from the hardware store.

"Can I see Stony?" she asked.

He shook his head soberly. "He'll be out of here sometime tonight. He'll ride out to see you. Wait until then." Apprehension filled her look, but, before she could speak, Crowe went on: "They're not goin' to break him out. I'm turnin' him loose."

"Then he didn't do it," Jo gasped, an inner hope lighting her eyes.

"Why are you askin' me that, Jo?" Crowe said gruffly. "You know he didn't."

She put her hands to her face then, and stood there sobbing quietly. The lawman crossed over to her, tilted her chin up.

"It's bad about Ralph, Jo," he said. "I'm sorry. You run along now and get on home. Take your outfit with you. I don't want them tanglin' in here tonight."

She asked him once again what he was planning to do, but he wouldn't tell her. When she had gone, he fortified himself with another drink, and again took his place at the door. The long shadows of the setting sun were fading to a quickly settling dusk. He sent across the street to the restaurant for Stony's supper, watched silently while his prisoner devoured the meal.

Stony was feeling better. He tried to talk to Crowe. But he soon gave up. Crowe felt no need of food for himself.

The lights had come on in the store windows when he went back into the office. He lighted the lantern just inside the cell-block, then lighted his office lamp, pulled down the shade, and went to his desk. In the drawer he found three Reward posters with Caden's picture on them, mates to the one O'Hara had burned. He laid one on his desk, then turned the chair to work the combination of the small safe behind him. He left the safe door open after he had taken out a folded sheet of paper from a small drawer inside.

This sheet was crumpled and dog-eared. He spread it flat on the desk and examined the writing on it. It was a note in Mike O'Hara's hand, a three-line message he had received months ago from the owner of the Golden Eagle. He took the stub of a pencil from his shirt pocket, turned the Reward notice face down, and began to write on the back of it.

It was laborious work to copy O'Hara's full, rounded style. He formed the letters lightly at first, then went over them again. Once he bent down and rubbed his hand along the dusty floor, then wiped a smudge across what he had written. After ten minutes he was satisfied with what he had done. Folding the Reward notice and putting it in his pocket, he replaced O'Hara's note in the safe, leaving its door open.

A ring of keys hung on a small nail behind the stove. Crowe took them down. Selecting one, he put it in his right boot.

His next job took him longer. Removing the cartridges from his .45, he pried the lead out of the cases of all five. It was trying work to replace the slugs again and make them fit, after he had emptied the powder from each shell. At last he finished, reloaded, and dropped the gun back into his holster. He threw the little mound of powder into the wood box, gave one look at the safe, standing open behind his desk, and then blew out the lamp and went out onto the street.

It took him ten minutes to find Fred Benson. When he did, he told him: "Fred, I've got a job for you. Get one of your men and come along down to the office."

Benson went across the street to the stable. In a minute he came out with Grant Schuler, his foreman. They arrived at the still dark office two minutes after Crowe had returned.

The sheriff took them inside and through into the cell-block without lighting the office lamp. Without a word, he led them to the end cell and unlocked the door. The light of the lantern hanging just inside the door to the office left this end cell in deep shadow.

"Fred, you and Grant go in there and set until I come back. It may be a half hour, maybe longer. Keep your ears unbuttoned, and don't spoil my play . . . no matter what happens." He stepped out until he could look into the cell nearest the office, where Stony Enders now stood, watching them. "The same goes for you, Stony. All of you act like you aren't even here."

"What the hell?"

"I don't know yet, Fred," Crowe cut in on Benson's puzzled query. "Only, remember . . . keep quiet, no matter what happens."

Crowe swung the door shut on them, but he did not lock it. Next, he went into his office, ran up the window shade. He brought his chair over to the window, and sat down. He sat there for twenty minutes, looking across the street, until he saw Hal Caden come out of the Golden Eagle and shoulder his way through the crowd. The sheriff then left the office, crossing the street up ahead of Caden.

He was waiting at the lunch counter doorway as Caden came along the walk. He stepped out in front of him.

"Have you got a minute before you feed,

116

Caden?"

"Sure," the other answered. "What'll you have?"

The sheriff nodded toward his office. "Follow me over to the office in a minute. It's important."

He moved on before the little gunman could make an answer. Crossing the street, he wanted to hurry, but forced himself to keep a slow, none-too-steady stride. He entered the office, lighted the lamp, and drew down the blind.

Caden came in half a minute later, his shifty gray eyes flashing a look about the small room, finally settling on the sheriff.

"Be with you in a minute," Crowe said, and lifted the lid off the sheet-iron stove. He bent down over the wood box, his right side turned away from Caden. When he straightened up again, his .45 rested in his palm.

"Reach, Four-Finger."

Caden's instinctive outward sweep of the hands was the first motion of a draw that suddenly terminated. For Walt Crowe's six-gun nosed up and centered on his shirt front. The gunman's hands went up, and his face took on a sneer.

"What's your play, Crowe?"

"You'll find out after you shed your hardware and pick yourself a cell. Shed it."

Caden hesitated, trying to understand. Then he reached down and unbuckled his belt, letting it slip down off his thighs and onto the floor. Crowe stepped forward and kicked the gun out of Caden's reach. Then he picked it up and put it in the safe at the back end of the office. He shut the safe door, and spun the combination.

Finished with that, Crowe jerked his head toward the cell-block door that stood open at the rear of the room. Caden went through it, and Crowe put him in the cell alongside Stony Enders.

As the door swung shut and the key grated in the lock, Caden turned, grasping the bars.

"Wait'll Mike hears about this," he snarled.

Crowe smiled broadly, reached into his pocket, and brought out the Reward notice. He handed it to Caden through the bars.

"Mike plays a pretty smart game," he said. "He sent that over an hour ago. For a hard-case, you're the easiest arrest I ever made."

Caden unfolded the sheet, smiling thinly as he looked at the face of it.

"I've seen this before. So's Mike."

"Turn it over."

Caden read:

CROWE ARREST CADEN FOR REDBURN MURDER LEAVE THE REST TO ME.

O'HARA

Caden's face took on a sickly pallor. "Let me out and give me my plow-handle, Crowe," he grated. "I'll kill that sidewinder."

Crowe laughed easily and shook his head. "Three thousand is as much as I make in three years, Caden." He leaned idly against the bars of the cell door, less than four feet from the stoop-shouldered little gunman, looking beyond and into the shadows where Fred Benson and Grant Schuler listened.

The look in Caden's eyes changed as he took in what the sheriff had done. His gray eyes hid his expression the next instant.

"You reckon Mike figures to take care of me tonight when he sends his mob over after Enders?"

Crowe shrugged. "That's how I figure it. You know too much."

Caden permitted himself a snort of disgust. "Mike should know. He paid me plenty for the job."

"I figured it was that way," Crowe drawled. "Well, guess I'll go out and set by the stove."

He turned and took one step away from the cell door before he felt the tug at his waist. He whirled in time to see Caden's hand dart back inside the bars again, holding his six-gun. With a leering grin, Caden raised the weapon and lined it at him.

"It's my turn now, Tin Star. Back up here. Make a move and I'll spill that whiskey out o' your guts."

Crowe swallowed thickly and said: "I was only doin' my duty, Caden. Don't forget that." He stepped in toward the door as he spoke. Caden reached through and lifted the keys off the ring at his belt.

"I never did play for a nickel pot, Lawman. I'm after O'Hara."

He was busy at the lock now. Abruptly they heard Stony Enders speaking: "It was you who killed Ralph Redburn, Caden?"

Caden paused a minute, looking through the grating at Enders. "The job was worth a thousand in gold. Mike made it easy."

"When I get out, I'm coming after you," Stony said, his voice brittle.

Caden had the door unlocked then, had pushed it open. His smile was wicked as he backed away, motioning Crowe to take his place in the cell. When he had locked the door and thrown the keys over against the far wall, he laughed quietly. "You won't follow anyone from where you're goin'," he told Enders.

Then he disappeared.

V

"Walt, I've got him in my sights through this window," came Fred Benson's voice. "Shall I let him have it?"

"Don't!" Crowe shouted. He heard Benson climb down off the cot.

"That was part of it?" Benson asked, pushing open the door to his own cell.

Crowe was sitting in the other cell, pulling off his boot. "It was," he said. When he had retrieved the key, and his boot was back on again, he reached through, unlocked the door, and stepped out beside them.

"What d'you aim to do, Walt?"

"You wait here a minute," Crowe said, going out into the office and bending over the safe. He worked the combination and had the safe open in a few seconds. He took out Caden's six-gun, thrust it in his holster, and went out the door.

The crowd in front of the swing doors at the Golden Eagle gave way before Crowe as he stepped up onto the walk. The men there had never before seen the look that was on their sheriff's face now.

The barroom was full, but at the back Crowe spotted Caden making his way toward the door of Mike O'Hara's office.

Leaving the door open, Caden stepped into the room and out of the sheriff's sight. Crowe heard their voices, O'Hara's and Caden's, and saw O'Hara get up from his desk and stride toward the door, reaching out to shut it.

Suddenly Mike paused. His lips came down in an ugly grimace, and he took a step back, forgetting now about the door. The next instant the big Irishman's hand was streaking for the six-gun at his thigh.

He moved with lightning quickness. The gun settled at his hip and lanced fire. The gun blast beat through the room, to bring it to a sudden silence.

All at once Caden staggered out into sight again, one claw-like hand clutching the spreading red splotch at his chest. In his other he held Walt Crowe's loadless .45.

As the sheriff watched, he saw the little gunman cast one brief glance down at his useless gun before his eyes smeared over. Caden fell out through the door, sprawling lifelessly.

O'Hara stepped over the gunman's body, holstering his Colt. He looked over toward the bar, signaling the man behind it.

"Cart this little sidewinder out o' here," he said crisply. Then his glance took in Walt

Crowe's presence, and he added: "Never mind, Charlie."

The two regarded each other for the space of a full second — O'Hara, the boss of Mound City, and Crowe, his hired lawman. But Mike O'Hara now saw at a glance that Crowe was changed, that he was no longer the drunken, weak-willed individual who had carried out his orders unquestioningly for ten years.

He hastened to speak. "Come into the office, Crowe."

"This'll do," Walt answered. "Mike, I'm arrestin' you for the murder of Ralph Redburn."

O'Hara's face flushed. His glance hardened. He jerked his head, to indicate Hal Caden's lifeless form on the floor. "There's your man, Crowe. Caden killed Redburn."

Crowe shook his head. "It won't work, Mike. I have two witnesses who heard Caden confess you paid him a thousand in gold to beef Redburn. Shed your hardware, Mike. You're under arrest."

The sheriff's words brought an angry murmur from the crowd.

Crowe saw the killing light that came then into Mike O'Hara's eyes. He knew what Mike was thinking of — the old Reward notice. If he killed Crowe, it would be all that was necessary to back his play.

O'Hara's casual glance went slowly over those in the smoke-fogged room. Yet Crowe saw his hand move before the eyes swung back again. His own hand swept up, feeling the cold slap of Caden's gun against his palm. The weapon lifted like a thing alive, in perfect balance.

Crowe thrilled to the lightness of the hammer's pull. The gun roared before he expected it, so light was the trigger. Mike O'Hara's huge bulk jerked as the lead caught him in the chest, yet his gun swept on up. The tremendous vitality of this man was hanging grimly on to send that one shot that would wipe out Walt Crowe.

The sheriff saw. Wildly he thumbed the hammer. He emptied the six-gun in a drumming trip-hammer series of blasts that became a prolonged roar in the confinement of the room. His second shot shattered Mike's wrist and tore the weapon from his hand. The third and fourth and fifth went after the first, closely grouped in the center of that broad expanse of white shirt front.

A smile crossed Mike O'Hara's face as life went out of him. Only Walt Crowe knew the meaning of that smile. Then Mike was falling, gone suddenly loose as the driving energy waned.

Crowe faced about, in time to see Fred Benson, Grant Schuler, and Stony Enders pushing their way toward him. He waited until Benson stood beside him.

"Fred, clean up this mess. I have a little job to do."

He went on back into Mike O'Hara's office, closing the door and locking it. He noted that the window shade was drawn before he commenced his search. It took him thirty minutes to find it, thirty minutes in which he disregarded the knocking at the door. When he finally found that Reward notice, wedged in the under side of the bottom drawer, he pulled it loose and touched a match to it. After the last glowing ash had winked out, he crumbled it down into O'Hara's ashtray and went over to open the door.

Stony Enders and Fred Benson were standing outside. On the floor at their feet was a wet spot ringing a darker one, where someone had tried to mop up Mike O'Hara's blood.

Crowe regarded Stony severely. "Why are you hangin' 'round?"

"I thought you might need some help, Walt."

"Help, hell! I've helped myself tonight. I told Jo you'd be ridin' out to see her." He paused a moment, smiling at the light that came into Stony Enders's eyes, then added gruffly: "Well . . . what're you waitin' on?"

MISSION TO THE GILAS

The original title of this story was "Gun-Mission to the Gilas." Jon Glidden completed it in late November, 1936, and sent it on to his agent, Marguerite E. Harper. His agent in turn sent it to Popular Publications where editor Mike Tilden bought it for *Star Western* on February 20, 1937. The author was paid $135. When the story was published in *Star Western* (6/37), its title had been changed to "A Lone Wolf Returns to the Gun-Pack." In the same issue was a story by Jon's brother, Fred, who wrote under the name Luke Short. Jon and his wife Dorothy (who was obviously the model for Judith Walton in this story) lived in an old adobe ranch house right across the road from Fred and his wife in the Pojoaque Valley, near Los Alamos. The text of this story is taken from the author's typescript but with his original title slightly modified.

I

In the ranch house office, the silence was awkward for all three. Fat Holden — the nickname was ironic — tilted his skeletal, scarecrow frame back in the broken-down swivel chair, hooked his spurs in the bottom, and stared with unseeing eyes before him. A slow flush of embarrassment crept beneath the deep tan of his face and spread up across a forehead beaded with perspiration. Judith Walton, erect in corduroy riding skirt and flannel shirt, stood nearby, anger glinting in the deep hazel of her eyes. She'd taken off her buckskin gloves and her small fists were clenched, knuckles white, as she defiantly faced the man who lounged against the adobe wall across the room. A sort of defiant indolence was in Luke McVickers's bearing as he met her glance with one equally firm, yet wholly impersonal. If he sensed the antagonism of the two confronting him, there was no betrayal of it on his sun-tanned, poker face.

Fat Holden coughed nervously and ripped away the silence: "So that's your answer, Luke?"

"That's my answer."

"You know what this means to us?" Holden asked without raising his eyes.

The man at the door shrugged. "Should I care?"

Judith Walton's quick indrawing of breath was plainly audible. A look of loathing momentarily marred the striking dark beauty of her face. When she spoke, her voice was husky with emotion.

"So you'll let it happen?" she asked. "Let it happen when you know we need your help? You'll stand by and watch us lose the Circle W? Luke, you can't."

Pausing, she saw instantly that Luke McVickers had lost none of his calm stolidity. She went on, a note of pleading in her voice, her eyes adding weight to the words: "Luke, can't you remember? Don't you remember how we . . . you and I . . . ?"

Luke McVickers chuckled softly and the insult brought Fat Holden's head up with a jerk. His eyes settled on McVickers in a winkless stare.

"We were just kids," Luke McVickers drawled. "I didn't know you Waltons then."

Fat Holden placed his outspread palms on the desk top and pushed himself slowly erect to stand beside Judith, saying: "I reckon you ought to pull out o' here now, Luke." His speech was clipped and hard with a thinly veiled menace.

"Not yet," Judith murmured. "Luke, you

must listen to me. You may be hard as rim-rock, as men say you are. I don't know what you've done during these seven years you've been away, or what you've made of yourself. . . ."

"That's easy to see, Judith," Holden cut in significantly, glancing at Luke's twin holsters. "Luke, you'd better leave."

"Stay out of this." Judith Walton laid a restraining hand on Holden's arm that was now hanging within finger spread of his six-gun. "Whatever you are, Luke, you're dead wrong about one thing. Dad didn't kill your father."

McVickers eased himself upright from his slouch against the wall. He was tall, deceptively so, for the breadth of powerful shoulders seemed to shorten him. Dust lay in the folds of his Levi's and blanket-lined canvas coat; his face was dark with beard-stubble and the blue eyes were sunken and red-rimmed from lack of sleep. His gun sheaths hung, loose and low, at his thighs, their rawhide thongs unlaced and hanging nearly to his boot tops.

Judith Walton's words for the moment erased any sign of fatigue he had shown. The mirthless smile that masked his thoughts faded.

"A hundred and thirty miles is a long way

to ride to be asked to throw in with the Waltons, Fat," he said, ignoring the girl. "Was that all you had on your mind when you wrote?"

"That was all." Holden's face had drained of its color and his eyes were focused at Luke McVickers's left shirt pocket. "You better get out!"

McVickers shrugged, turned toward the door, and opened it. Stepping through, he paused long enough to ask: "Sure you don't want to ride with me, Fat? There's fewer polecats north o' here."

Fat Holden choked out his answer. "By God, Luke, you clear out!"

McVickers was gone then, and the last fleeting glimpse they had of his face was one in which his smile returned.

Judith crossed the room, went out the door, and stood to watch him stride out across the yard to the hitch rail. A moment later Holden followed and stood at her elbow. The dry chill of a mid-morning breeze fanned briskly the length of the porch in stimulating contrast to the warmth indoors.

Holden shifted uneasily and said: "I'll gut-shoot that coyote the first time I lay eyes on him again."

Judith shook her head slowly. "You'd be

dead before your gun was clear, Fat. He's
right, too. He really thinks Dad did kill old
Jeff McVickers."

"He's too bull-headed to. . . ."

"No, it's not that," she interrupted. "He's
strong enough to pick his own trail and follow it. But I'm glad Dad wasn't here. Luke
would have killed him."

They were silent then, watching as Luke
wheeled his tired, sweat-caked sorrel from
the hitch rail and headed off down the lane
that ran past the barn. Judith sighed wearily,
and Holden, turning to look at her, saw that
her eyes were moist.

She murmured: "Fat, there goes a man."

Neither Fat nor Judith saw, a few minutes
later, the cowpuncher who had hired out to
the Circle W under the name of Tade Barlow
edge casually around the corner of the
house, away from the door of the ranch office. He had heard enough, and now a single
purpose moved him. He made his way aim-
lessly toward the corral. Once there, he
flashed a glance back toward the low-lying
adobe house. For a moment Barlow's eyes
were hate-filled; his hand dropped downward to the butt of his Colt. Then, dismiss-
ing what was in his mind, he took down the
top bar of the corral and went in to snake
out a thick-barreled buckskin. In five min-

utes he had saddled the mare and was riding northeast, angling off to the left of the trail where he could still see Luke McVickers.

A mile from the Circle W, Barlow rode down over the lip of a draw. Once out of sight he rammed in his spurs and sent the buckskin into a swinging run. He held the pace for ten minutes before he angled toward the east to parallel the trail McVickers had taken. A half hour later he slid the lathered mare to a stop at the foot of a towering butte that prominently dominated the broad sweep of rolling range.

There, sitting the saddle with his sheepskin collar turned up against the chill air, another rider waited for him. At a word from Barlow, they rode to the base of the massive piled rock, ground-haltered their horses, and started climbing up through the time-eroded boulders. It was hard work, for ice and snow in the sunless shadows made the footing uncertain. But in ten minutes they lay, winded and perspiring, on a narrow ledge fifty feet above the trail that cut, string-straight, across the bunch grass prairie to lose itself toward the east.

Presently a rider topped a hogback and rode slowly toward them, two miles out on the trail. Barlow spoke gruffly. "McVickers is played out. Said he'd been ridin' for two nights and a day."

The man beside him, taller and thicker than Barlow, grunted and was silent for a long minute. Then he asked: "You sure it's him? I'm havin' to take your word for it."

"Hell, yes," Tade Barlow countered, running his palm over a two-inch scar that drew a line through the beard stubble at his jaw. "I don't forget easy."

Silence hung heavily as they waited. Finally Luke McVickers was close enough so that the sound of the sorrel's iron-shod hoofs, striking rock on the trail, came up to them distinctly.

"Any chance he'll change his mind and go back to the Circle W?" asked Barlow's companion.

"No. Not unless he'd ride back to cut down on Holden."

A slow smile drew down the tall man's thin lips and he sighed in satisfaction as he looked below again. 100 yards out on the trail, Luke McVickers rode wearily, letting his body weave loosely to the movement of the walking gelding.

"Brown Stetson, gray canvas coat, black Levi's. Silver *conchas* on his belt," muttered the tall man, edging forward a little to keep McVickers in sight. "Can't see his cutters, though. . . ."

"Bone-handled," Barlow put in. "That is, they were two years ago."

The other gave no indication that he had heard, but went on: "We could doctor up that blaze-faced sorrel colt Bob Simmons broke last week to look a lot like McVickers's bronc'."

"I doubt it. There ain't a horse in Kettle Basin as big as that sorrel down there."

As Barlow spoke, he made a stealthy movement. The man lying beside him turned his head quickly, and lunged the next instant. Two seconds later, he had the smaller man pinned under him, his right hand locked about the Colt .45 Barlow held, wedging its blunt snout down against the rock face of the ledge.

For three second there was a tensely unmoving struggle for the possession of the weapon. At length the tall man got to his knees with the Colt pressed firmly into the flesh at Barlow's throat.

Breathing heavily, he muttered: "I ought to kill you for that, Tade."

Barlow's muttered curses ceased long enough for him to whisper: "Goddlemightly, don't touch that trigger."

The big man shifted his glance downward. For two minutes he sat astride Barlow without moving the six-gun, waiting until

McVickers had drawn away down the trail. Then, satisfied that he could not be heard, he said in a normal tone: "I reckon you ain't aimin' to live long, Tade."

The little gunman's face was ashen and he spoke without moving so much as his lips. "Take that cutter away. A whisper'll drop the hammer."

Slowly the big man rose and stood over Barlow. "I figured you'd try a double-cross someday," he mused.

Barlow sat up, his courage visibly returning. "I'm not crossin' you. But I'm damned if I let the one man I've been huntin' for two years ride right under my nose . . . alive. You told me I could have McVickers."

"You can." The other chuckled dryly, his manner abruptly changing. He shrugged and tossed the Colt to Barlow. "Only we're playin' this another way, Tade. You ride to the Box M, and tell Bob Simmons to blot out the white patch on that sorrel colt's face. Tobacco juice would do it. Then ride back to the Circle W before Holden misses you. Right now I'm ridin' for Red Dog . . . to see this McVickers."

II

Red Dog sprawled its array of red adobe buildings over both banks of a dry wash scarcely two miles out from the low-lying green foothills of the Gilas. The craggy peaks in the distance were snow-mantled, yet here in Kettle Basin there was little sign of winter. Aside from the thin plumes of wood smoke that thickened the dust haze over the single street, Red Dog's glaring ugliness was the same as when Luke McVickers had last seen it.

His glance shuttled from side to side as he rode toward Holloway's livery barn. Seven years had worked no change here, beyond the fact that the Straight Flush was boarded up, with a For Rent sign painted on its crumbling front wall.

At the stable he dismounted and turned the gelding over to a gangling youth he did not recognize, giving him instructions to grain and rub down the animal. Then, throwing his saddle roll over his shoulder, he walked stiffly across the street and into the Mile High House.

At the desk in the small lobby, he recognized the elderly hotel owner who dozed behind it in a chair. Stewpan Donnelly roused himself, looked at McVickers without recognition, and got out of his chair to shove a tattered register forward across the desk top.

McVickers signed it **Abe Holeman, Tuba**

137

City, Ariz.

"All I want's a bed," he said. "I'm turnin' in now."

Stewpan's brows raised a trifle in surprise, but he turned with a shrug and took down a key from the board behind his chair. "Dollar and a half, stranger."

McVickers paid ungrudgingly and followed him up the rickety stairs and down the length of the upstairs hall. At the end room Stewpan threw open a door, waved casually through it.

"Not much, but she'll do," he said amiably. "Holler if you want more blankets."

Throwing his roll on the one chair, McVickers sat on the bed and casually examined the room, as the oldster clumped back down the hall. The shade at the window was torn; a neat bullet hole centered the lower rectangle of wavy dirty glass. A chest of drawers, a basin and pitcher, the chair, and the bed were the room's only furnishings.

McVickers sighed, lifted one foot, and tugged at his boot. At that instant he heard a light step in the hall, caught a hint of movement in the doorway at the limit of his vision, and threw himself backward onto the bed, rolling onto his left side. Before his shoulder had touched the mattress, his right hand had flicked out a Colt .38 and lined it at a figure in the doorway.

The man standing there made no move; his thumbs remained hooked loosely in his sagging, shell-studded belt. McVickers felt a little ridiculous and got up slowly from the bed, keeping the Colt in his hand. The intruder smiled thinly, stepped inside the room, and closed the door.

"Are you McVickers?" he asked.

"Keep on talkin'," Luke drawled.

The other's glance shifted to the weapon. "I can talk better without lookin' into your plow handle."

McVickers dropped the .38 back into its holster but remained silent, examining the man who confronted him. Black, skin-tight pants fitted into fine boots, a dark red flannel shirt showed from under a brown leather vest, and twin ivory-handled Colt .45s completed an outfit that was obviously expensive. The smile held on the dark, well-molded face until the man, at length, spoke again.

"Don't know me, do you, McVickers? I'm Ren Emrath."

The name brought up an indefinable antagonism within McVickers, yet he put it down. He answered evasively: "Should that mean somethin' to me?"

For a moment a faint touch of surprise crossed the stranger's features. Then he smiled again, easily. "I'm owner of your father's old outfit, the Box M."

McVickers's brows came up, and, when he spoke, his voice was purposely casual: "Never did hear who bought the outfit from the bank."

"I came up to chew the fat with you, McVickers."

Luke shook his head and the hard lines came back into his tan face. "Not now. I'm due for some sleep. See you later."

"It won't take a minute," Emrath put in quickly, as McVickers let himself down on the bed and started pulling off his boots.

"No," Luke said flatly.

"I'm hirin' men."

"I'm not for hire. I'm headin' north to-night."

"What brought you down here?"

McVickers stared openly at the other for a long moment before he answered: "That's twice you've dealt off the bottom of the deck, Emrath. The first time was in comin' in here without knockin'. Now you're askin' me somethin' that's none of your damned business. Am I goin' to have to throw you out?"

Emrath overlooked the insult. A devilish

light of laughter was mirrored in his black eyes. "You're just as proddy as they claim," he said. "I can use you. Would you like to even things up with the Circle W?"

Luke feigned surprise. "Did anyone ever tell you I needed help?" he asked. Abruptly a subtle warning told him that there was more to be learned from the man who faced him, so he added: "How do you figure I could even things with Fred Walton?"

"I'm runnin' Fred Walton's brand off this range. You can help me do it."

"What's between you and the Circle W?" McVickers put the question without committing himself.

"Didn't Fat Holden tell you this mornin'?"

McVickers's face became an unreadable mask, hiding the astonishment he felt in learning that Emrath knew of his visit at the Circle W. For a long moment he debated his answer, finally gave it directly: "Holden did say a few things about the Box M. Now let's have your side of the story."

Emrath shook his head and smiled. "Not till I know how you stand in this. Are you goin' to throw in with Holden?"

"I'll cut him down the first time I see him," Luke breathed, spacing his words carefully.

Emrath was convinced. His expression abruptly changed to one of geniality. "I'll pay you a hundred and fifty a month, beginnin'. . . ."

"Did I say my guns were for hire?" McVickers cut in. "Let's hear your story first."

Shrugging his broad shoulders, Emrath told him: "I reckon you know all there is to it. The Jackson Draw water hole was dynamited one night last week. One of my riders saw the polecat who did it and threw some lead at him. Killed his horse but the rider got away in the dark. The dead bronc' was branded Circle W."

"How come you had a rider at the water hole?" Luke asked.

"Three weeks ago Walton drove a bunch of cattle through it and muddied it up so's it wasn't fit to use for days," Emrath explained. "Since then I've kept a man up in the rocks with a Winchester."

Luke, who had been staring at him pointedly, said: "Sounds a lot like seven years ago. That was before your time in this country." He added: "It was in a fight over that water that Fred Walton cut down on my father."

Emrath nodded. "I know. I've heard about it. There didn't seem. . . ."

"It's a damned funny thing," Luke interrupted, "that the two outfits ever fought over that water hole. Neither one of you could do without it. Fred Walton would lose at least a third of his north range if he didn't have it. The Box M would be as bad off without it, since you haven't any other water within fifteen miles."

"Can't figure it out myself, McVickers. Walton is just plain ornery. I've tried to get along with him, but he's as forked as a snake's tongue."

"I know, I know," mused Luke. "That's what my old man said about him when the trouble started. There was a time when they were good friends."

Emrath had been eyeing McVickers fixedly. When he had finished, he said bluntly: "It's worth a thousand in gold for me to see Fred Walton cut to doll rags. Will you take on the job?"

McVickers's surprise was genuine as he drawled: "So it's gone that far, has it?"

"A thousand more if Holden accidentally cashes in his chips," Emrath went on intently, a clear hard hatred making his lean handsome face ugly.

"That would be a pleasure," McVickers breathed. "But what makes you think I'd hire out to kill a man?"

Ren Emrath waved a hand carelessly. "I've heard about you, that's all."

McVickers raised his brows questioningly, then stretched, and slowly rose to stand by the bed. He lazily kicked his boots away from in front of him and turned to face the other, standing with feet spread a little apart. "When do you want your answer?" he asked.

"Now," Emrath answered. "Will you, or won't you?"

"How about the girl?" Luke asked, striving to keep his voice at an even pitch.

"Judith?" Emrath asked. He smiled and raised his brows in an expression that was insulting in its implications. "If I get the spread, I get the girl, don't I?"

"What does she say about that?"

"What the hell do I care? There's one way of makin'. . . ."

Ren Emrath saw it coming and made a stab at his six-gun. But before his outspread fingers reached his .45 the full force of McVickers's whip-like blow caught him under the side of his jaw, the impact making a *thud* in the momentary silence. Emrath crashed heavily into the wall, caught himself, and lunged. McVickers stepped back, feinted with his left, and drove a smashing right uppercut at the other's face. The blow caught Emrath behind the ear and his lunge became all at once a sprawl as he went loose and dropped onto the floor. He lay there without moving.

McVickers, breathing heavily, turned the tall man over on his back. Taking a firm hold on the leather vest and shirt, he lofted him from the floor, dragged him through the door, and down the short length of the hall.

It took all his strength to heave the limp form down over the first step. He stood watching while the rancher sprawled and rolled down the flight of stairs, ending in a motionless heap at the bottom.

Steps sounded in the small lobby below. Stewpan Donnelly came into view, hurriedly crossed over, and kneeled beside Emrath. Then he looked up and saw McVickers.

"What the hell are you doin'?" he bawled.

"I found that skunk in my room!" McVickers called down.

"This is Ren Emrath!" Stewpan shouted.

"I didn't know they named 'em down here," McVickers replied, and went back to his room.

It took him exactly forty seconds to move the chest of drawers in front of the door and fall to sleep on the bed. After five minutes of pounding at the barricaded door,

Stewpan Donnelly trudged back down the stairs. . . .

III

Luke McVickers roused into complete wakefulness. His room was in total darkness. He climbed out of bed feeling a new freshness in his stiffened muscles, and walked to the open window. A glance up at the stars told him that it was past midnight. Cursing softly in surprise, he hurriedly pulled down the blind and lighted the lamp that stood on the chest of drawers before the door. Then as he recalled what had happened since his coming to Kettle Basin, he chuckled grimly. Now there was no need for hurry.

"A shave, some chow, and I'll ride," he mused, half aloud. In the utter stillness of the old building the sound of his voice startled him.

By the light of the lamp, and using the cracked mirror on the wall, he lathered his face and began to shave. He felt a distinct pleasure at the way Ren Emrath's visit had terminated. Recalling the purpose of the visit sobered him, and for a moment his thoughts ran back over pictures of the past.

There was the Jackson Draw water hole, with his father's bullet-riddled body lying in the mud alongside the dynamited reservoir that had bred such bitterness between the Circle W and the Box M. Then Fred Walton's previous denial that he had dynamited it and his threat against Jeff McVickers's life on the day before the shooting. Foreclosure on the Box M by the bank after McVickers's death. And himself, a strapping youth of eighteen, as he confronted Fred Walton a week after the funeral, daring him to draw and sling lead, but only to face the soul-tearing humiliation of having Walton take up his dare and outdraw him, then refuse to shoot a helpless kid!

After Sheriff Thomas's warning for him either to stop his talk against Walton or leave town, there followed days of riding, with loyal Fat Holden at his side. But his smoldering temper involved him in a dozen brawls and four killings. Holden grew disgusted, and finally broke with the son of Jeff McVickers.

"When you get that loco streak worn out of you, let me know," Fat Holden had said. "I'm headin' back to Kettle Basin for a job."

Holden's departure had sobered him. Since then, for seven years, he had held down twenty jobs in twenty counties in five states, neither seeking trouble nor avoiding it, using when necessary that terrific gun magic he had perfected.

Never once had he heard of Holden — until three days ago when he had received his friend's message, a plea for help. It was a ruse that had brought him back to Kettle Basin, for he had not learned of Holden's whereabouts until the morning of his arrival. News that Fat was rodding the Circle W revived once more that smoldering hatred for Fred Walton, and he had ridden on, determined to meet the rancher and have it out with him. But Walton was absent, helping his men drive a herd out of a snowed-under pasture in the hills.

Holden had minced no words. Even now, Luke gave him credit for being outspoken. Would Luke throw in with the Walton outfit and help run Ren Emrath off the range? Masking his feelings, Luke had gradually pried out of Holden the story of a revived war over the Jackson Draw water hole. It was a repetition of the events of seven years ago. Fred Walton, to all appearance a reasonable and fine man, was again attempting to drive the Box M off the range by depriving the spread of water. Why? Luke could not even now answer this question.

Since seeing Ren Emrath, Luke's desire to take a hand in this had left him. Let these two curly wolves fight it out between them.

If both stopped lead, then so much the better. Then, abruptly, Luke knew that this was not his reason for pulling out. The haunting picture of Judith Walton's loveliness and the fear of hurting her had actually convinced him that he must leave and let matters take their own course. For a moment he was filled with a regret that fate had so surely put her beyond his reach. It would take more than seven years to change his feelings for her.

He strapped up his saddle roll viciously, knowing that the only thing that would give him peace of mind would be to put Kettle Basin far behind him. He left his room by way of the window. Stewpan Donnelly would be waiting for him downstairs, curious and belligerent, and Luke was in no frame of mind to face the irritable old codger.

He dropped lightly down into the alley that ran alongside the hotel, hid his saddle roll in an empty rain barrel near the front of the weathered frame building, then sauntered out onto the deserted street.

The air was chill and his breath showed in a smoky fog made eerily blue by the cold star-studded night. Only two pale rectangles of light showed along the crooked length of the street. One would be coming from the

Glory Hole saloon, while the one this side of it he knew was the shack of Ling's Lunch. He walked on and entered Ling's shack and found the yellow little Chinaman dozing behind his counter.

Ling started from his sleep as the door banged shut. His sleepy almond eyes opened and a grin of instant recognition broke the smoothness of his yellow face.

"Howdee, Mist' Luke! Damn' long time no see!"

"Howdy, Ling," Luke greeted him, pleased at the other's welcome. "Can you rustle me some chow?"

Ling's smile faded and his forehead all at once wrinkled into a frown as he thought of something. He leaned forward over the counter, said in a high whisper: "Sure, I catch chow. But watch out . . . Box M boys raise plenty hell w'en they see you."

"How come, Ling?"

Ling shrugged expressively on his way back to his kitchen. "I no tell no more. But they mad as plenty hell."

Luke laughed, wondering how it was that the news of his encounter with Emrath could have reached Ling's ears. Ling came out of his kitchen with a bowl of soup. Before Luke had finished it, a platter of food rested on the counter before him. He decided to wait until he had finished eating before quizzing Ling.

He had nearly finished his meal when he heard the door open behind him. Turning to inspect the newcomer, Luke found himself staring into the muzzle of a leveled .45. Behind it stood Sheriff Len Thomas. His face was old and grizzled and a little blanched, yet in his hard blue eyes flashed an unmistakable warning.

Luke slowly turned on the stool to face the lawman, edging his hands upward. He heard a sound from the kitchen and his glance shuttled back to find Fat Holden standing at the rear of the counter, a sawed-off shotgun resting in the crook of his left arm.

"Ling, you reach over and lift out his irons," Thomas ordered. "Luke, I'll cut you off pocket high if you make a move."

"You should've brought along more help, Len," Luke drawled, as Ling followed the sheriff's instructions. "Mind tellin' me what . . . ?"

"Hell, no, I won't waste my wind. You climb off that stool and head for the lockup. On the way make a break for it, if you want. I'd sure like an excuse for beefin' you."

Holden advanced from the rear of the shack, and, when Luke encountered his glance, he read the danger there. That, in itself, was sobering. He rose and stepped out the door and down the walk, puzzled to see that several mounted riders were waiting in front of the jail down the street. Thomas shuffled along beside him, prodding him in the ribs with the .45.

After a few paces the lawman spoke up: "Damn it, you ain't goin' to let us take you, are you, McVickers? For God's sake, make a break so's we can get this over with."

"Easy, Len," Holden spoke up from behind. "We're doin' this upright. It won't take more'n a day to try him and hang him."

Luke was silent. It occurred to him that Ren Emrath might possibly have died as a result of his fall down the hotel stairs, but at once he dismissed the thought, knowing that Fat Holden would not back the sheriff for that reason. They crossed the street to the jail, the riders shifting sullenly aside to allow them to pass. In the dim light that shone from the jail office window Luke recognized the Circle W jaw brands on the horses. More puzzled than ever, he waited until the office door had closed behind him.

"Fat, I'm askin' you to tell me what this is all about," he said.

Holden deliberately leaned his shotgun against the wall, and then straightened up to his full gaunt height, his eyes smoky and bitter.

"Len, he's askin' us what he's here for. Shall I tell him?"

"Sure, go ahead," Thomas answered, disgust in his tone.

With the quickness of a striking rattler, Fat Holden swung his fist. Luke dodged, but the blow caught him on the side of the head and threw him back against the sheriff's desk. He crouched, ready to spring back at Holden, but the lawman whipped up his six-gun.

"Lock him up, Len," Holden breathed. "In another minute I'll lose my temper and use this scatter-gun."

Len Thomas unlocked the heavy wooden door to the cell-block, took down a lantern from a peg on the wall of the little office, lighted it, and led the way. He opened the door to the middle of the three cells, swung it shut after Luke had entered. Holden followed, bringing in a chair and his shotgun.

He seated himself on the chair, leaned back against the wall to one side of the office door, and drawled: "Leave the lantern here, Len. I'm guardin' this sidewinder till daylight."

The sheriff set the lantern on the floor, and shook his head slowly. "I won't arrest you, if you let that gun off accidental-like, Fat," he commented. "Hell, to think it had to be Fred!" He slammed the door behind him and they could hear the clump of his boots as he crossed the office and shouted to the men outside.

Luke waited until he had made and lighted a cigarette, then addressed Holden: "What's happened to Fred Walton, Fat?"

The lean foreman of the Circle W made no answer. For two full minutes the silence remained unbroken, until at length Holden eased his chair to the floor and took out tobacco and makings.

Luke ventured another remark: "I've been asleep since two o'clock yesterday afternoon, Fat."

Holden gave him a long look and muttered: "Why waste your wind, Luke? We even found your sorrel all lathered up down in the corral at the end o' town."

"That's news," Luke mused. "He must be plumb wore out after the ridin' he's had the last three days."

Holden kept silent. Luke made and smoked his second cigarette. The air in the room was raw with the cold and Luke regretted that he had left his coat hanging back in the lunch shack. At length Holden, feeling the chill, rose and paced back and forth the length of the room, carrying his shotgun under his arm.

He stopped his pacing in front of Luke's cell, looked at his prisoner a moment, and said in an even voice: "I wonder what old Jeff McVickers would say if he knew his son shot a man in the back, without even lettin' him go for his iron?"

Luke, sitting on the cot in the cell got to his feet, came to the bars, and clenched them in his fists, meeting Holden's stare. "Fat, I didn't kill Fred Walton. Forty minutes ago I was asleep in my room."

For a moment anger blazed up in Holden's eyes again, then died as he chuckled dryly: "That's what I can't figure about you, Luke. I'd have thought you could hide your sign better. We already seen Stewpan, and he told us you climbed out the window."

"Sure," Luke agreed. "I left my room just before I showed up at Ling's. I didn't want to have to tell Stewpan why I threw Emrath down the stairs. Maybe you'd like to hear why I did."

"Let it go. Let it go," Holden muttered, waving his hand in disgust. He turned and went back to resume his seat in the chair.

Clearly Luke realized the futility of words. Unknowingly he had shattered his only alibi by climbing out the window of the Mile

High House. Holden, already bitter against him for his refusal to help the Circle W, was now fanatical in his hatred.

An hour passed. The raw cold of the cell room tightened Luke's muscles until he was stiff. He rose from the cot once to wrap the one thin blanket about him, but decided that it would serve its purpose better in cutting off the draft from the barred window above his head. He stuffed it into the opening, tying it as best he could around the bars.

Holden watched him suspiciously at first but soon satisfied his curiosity and resumed his vacant gazing at the floor ahead of his chair.

Before he sat down again, Luke asked another question: "Where did it happen, Fat?"

Fat shook his head. He laughed once, dryly, but made no reply.

IV

Luke was dozing when he heard the office door open. He lifted his head and saw Judith Walton standing in the door's rectangle. She closed it softly behind her and leaned back against it, giving no indication that she saw Holden in his chair beside her, but staring, wide-eyed, at Luke. In the lamplight

156

her dark brown hair took on a tint of deep gold. A heavy coat gave nothing but a hint of the roundness of her slender body.

Luke came slowly up off the cot and stepped forward to stand by the door.

"Judith," he began. "Maybe you. . . ."

He stopped then, seeing that she had taken her right hand from the pocket of her coat. In that hand she held a double-barreled Derringer. A twisted smile broke the somberness of her olive-colored face as she stepped forward toward his cell.

"Go ahead, Judith," Holden drawled. "I've been savin' him for you."

Luke breathed deeply, feeling the sudden coolness of sweat on his brow. He spoke automatically, without thinking, and the steadiness of his voice startled him.

"I'm sorry to hear about your dad, Judith."

A mirthless smile lit up her face as she breathed contemptuously: "To think I'd ever love a man like you."

It was strange that at this moment Luke should find cause for elation in her words. But there was no denying it. "Hearin' you say that makes up for a lot o' things, Judith."

He saw all at once that she was not looking at him. Her glance ran past and above him and the next moment her eyes dilated with fear. She screamed, and he whirled in time to see the blanket drop out of the window.

Quickly as thought, he knew what was coming and threw himself to the floor. A split second later a terrific blast shook the little building.

Luke felt the light beat of a weight on his boots, as though someone had tapped him on the heels. The next instant he was crawling to the back wall of the cell, edging close up to it beneath the window.

Holden's steps sounded behind at the cell door and Luke turned in time to see him poke his shotgun through the bars, aiming at the window. A second later his gun thundered out a double charge of buckshot that ricocheted shrilly off into the darkness outside.

"Bushwhacker!" Holden rasped, then bent down over Judith who lay huddled on the floor.

"Is she hurt, Fat?" Luke came to stand at the front of the cell.

"Fainted," Holden told him. "I'll get some water." He was gone then, running through the door and on into the office.

Luke looked down at Judith and what he found was reassuring. The double blast from the killer's shotgun at the window had plowed into the floor to one side of her. His blood ran cold when he saw how unerringly accurate that gun had been, exactly in line with where he had been standing.

Remembering the tug at his foot, he looked down to see that the leather above the heel of his right boot had been grooved by two pellets from the buckshot charge. Something in the shadow on the floor by his foot took his attention and the next instant he recognized it. He leaned over to pick up the Derringer Judith had been holding in her hand. Breaking it open, he found it loaded.

From out front he heard Holden crossing through the office, and he hastily thrust the wicked little weapon into his hip pocket.

Holden dampened his bandanna in the dipperful of water he carried, knelt beside Judith, and placed it on her forehead. Her eyes opened. With a quick effort she pushed herself up.

"Luke! Is Luke all right?"

Fat Holden nodded soberly and pointed to the cell. Judith saw Luke standing there and began to sob quietly. From the office came the sounds of hurrying feet, and Sheriff Thomas appeared in the doorway.

"What happened, Holden?"

"It's all over, Len. Someone tried a bush-whack through the window. Put a couple of the boys out there with rifles and tell 'em to keep everyone away from here. Luke McVickers is standin' trial."

The sheriff closed the door and left the office. Luke looked down to see that Judith's color had returned. She was quiet now. When his glance raised, he caught a puzzled frown on Holden's face.

"I'm askin' you once more to tell me what happened tonight," Luke said. "Do you know now I didn't kill Fred Walton?"

Fat sighed wearily, scratched his head, and muttered: "This has got me whipped."

"What are you saying, Luke?" Judith asked in an awed whisper.

"That I wasn't anywhere near the Circle W tonight. That I don't even know what happened to your father."

"It wasn't you?"

"No."

"That lie don't hold, Luke," Holden cut in. "You know damn' well I saw you. I was standin' right beside Fred when you let him have it. I don't fool easy. The light on the porch was good enough so that I could see. Those silver *conchas* on your belt and your bone-handled cutters gave you away."

"Maybe you were supposed to see things,"

Luke retorted, thinking aloud. "If I wanted to cut down on a man, I'd meet him fair and give him an even draw. You say Fred Walton didn't have a chance."

Holden gave a negative gesture. "Not a chance. Besides that, one of the boys down at the barn had a good look at your sorrel." He paused a moment, then added with conviction: "You're standin' trial, Luke."

"Who else could it be?" Judith asked.

"If I stand trial, there'll be a mob to hang me," Luke broke in. "So I'm not standin' trial, Fat."

Holden smiled confidently and turned away, reaching across to where he had left his shotgun.

"Look over here a minute, Fat."

The other faced about and caught the glint of reflected lamplight from the Derringer McVickers held in his hand. Judith took one backward step to stand beside Holden.

"It wouldn't take much urgin' to make me squeeze the trigger," Luke said. "Turn around and back up to these bars, Fat. Besides, you forgot to load that smoke pole."

For a long moment, Holden did not move. Luke's hand was rock steady. Gradually the other's color left him, and, when he spoke, it was in a hoarse whisper: "I think you'd do it."

"He would," Judith gasped.

With that, Holden came across to the cell, turned around, and in two seconds had been relieved of the .45 in the holster at his thigh.

"Both of you stand over in that far corner," Luke ordered. "I'm goin' to blow the lock off this door and ride out o' here."

It was obvious that their momentary doubt as to his guilt had now left them. Holden's eyes were hard with a quiet fury as he backed into the corner. Judith's features were beautiful, even though they registered nothing but contempt for him.

He spoke again, saying: "Before I leave, there's something I'd like to say . . . a thing or two I'd like you to do. In the first place find out what caliber bullet killed Fred Walton. Nine chances out of ten it was a Forty-Five. You know I carry Thirty-Eights. Next, it wouldn't hurt to look around out back and see if there is any sign of the ranny that blew this hole in the floor. You might also have a talk with the livery stable boy and see who it was took my sorrel out tonight." He paused, giving his words time to sink in. "Now, plug up your ears because I'm on my way."

With that he raised Holden's .45 and

thumbed two shots at the solid lock of the cell door. The impact of the bullets left the iron grating standing open an inch. A shove, and he walked out into the corridor, saying: "Hope I don't have to throw lead at any of your riders outside, Judith."

"You're a killer, Luke. They'll get you."

Her words took away any shred of warmth left in him. When he edged through the door into the dark office, he was without nerves — a hard, bitter fighting machine. He found his two .38s in one of the drawers of the sheriff's desk, thrust Holden's .45 into his belt, and took his own guns in his hands.

The street was in total darkness as he opened the door and flashed a glance outside. Strangely enough the guard he had expected to find there was not in sight, and the fact of the man's absence sent a flood of wariness through him. Three saddled horses stood at the hitch rail and he picked the biggest.

Two strides took him across the walk. The animals shied in fright at his swift approach. As he vaulted into the saddle, he caught a hint of movement at the far corner of the jail wall. His .38 lanced flame as he snapped a shot high above the line of a rifle barrel edging around the corner to cover him. It threw the guard off his aim and gave

McVickers enough time to wheel the horse and ram home the spurs.

Then he was away, down the street. A sharp *crack* sounded out; he felt a quick tug at his left shoulder the same instant, and knew that the guard's bullet had found its mark.

The street twisted, cutting him off from any immediate danger. He felt confident that he would have at least a five-minute start on his pursuers. The street had been practically deserted as he looked down it, and he reasoned that most of the Circle W riders in town had stabled their horses.

He headed west out of town, followed the trail that would take him past Twin Tent Butte for three miles before he cut off from it across rock toward the north. At that point he reined in, listened for ten long seconds, and was rewarded by nothing but the howl of a coyote as it lifted its voice in an eerie chant. Judging that he had at least another hour and a half of darkness, he rode on at a fast trot, saving his horse, confident that those behind would not find where he had left the trail until daybreak.

In forty minutes he was well into the foothills. He rode steadily on toward the mountain shadows, and, when the full dawn came, he was punishing his horse over rocky ground. The cold chilled him, and with this came an added discomfort — a dull throb in his shoulder. He rode on until he came to the thin trickle of a clear stream and spent ten minutes washing the wound and bandaging it. The bullet had gone clean through the muscle above his collar bone. Although it was not serious, the constant movement of his shoulder in riding set up a throbbing ache. He went on, ignoring it.

The sun was an hour beyond its zenith when Luke McVickers dismounted in a stand of cedar on a slope that rose 200 yards in back of the Box M ranch buildings. He knew every foot of this country and had picked his way here carefully, certain that he had not been seen. Three hours had been spent that morning covering his trail over rocky ground. Unless he had calculated wrongly, he had left no sign that would show where his goal lay.

Looking down now on the layout that had been his home for eighteen years, he was touched with definite regret. The memory of his feeling as he had last seen the place came back, yet he found it strangely foreign to him now. The thought startled him. Oddly enough, he had lost his old bitterness.

The thing that had led him here at once crystallized in his mind. Miles back on the trail he had suddenly realized that the blasting charge of buckshot through the jail window, coupled with Fred Walton's mysterious death, had re-arranged things. He now had conclusive proof of Fred Walton's innocence. Walton had obviously been shot down in cold blood. The one man who most wanted his death was Ren Emrath. Again, no Circle W rider could possibly be responsible for the attempt on his life at the jail. That was not Fat Holden's way; neither could it be Judith's, no matter how much loathing she felt for him.

There was only one answer, and he was here to discover it. It was a long chance he was taking, yet he knew of no other way to go about it. He would hide until dark, and then go to meet Emrath for the showdown.

He made himself as comfortable as he could, using a rawhide saddle thong for a sling for his arm. He stayed close to his horse, a rangy, strong brown gelding ready to stop him from nickering if the occasion arose.

The Box M presented quite a complete layout as he examined it. There was a new wagon shed, the roof of the old well house had been renewed, and the frame house itself showed signs of having been repaired. Whatever his shortcomings, Emrath had not let the spread run down. The surroundings made the place more attractive than most of the ranches in this country, for Jeff McVickers had purposely built his home in the foothills, since his range ran well to the craggy slopes of the Gila foothills. Seven miles to the south lay the buildings of the Circle W, reached by the trail that cut off across the valley directly opposite the point where Luke was hiding.

It was late afternoon when Luke saw something on that trail that brought him immediately alert. A rider appeared around the bend in the trail and rode at a pounding run toward the Box M.

In front of the house he slid his chestnut to a quick stop, threw himself out of the saddle, and ran toward the house. Luke glued his eyes to the spot, sensing that the rider's errand was important, and at the same time at the back of his mind grew a certainty that he had seen this man before. However, the distance had been too great to recognize him, as he sat quietly waiting developments below.

They were not long in coming. In two minutes, the short, slight figure of the rider reappeared, walking toward his horse, and beside him strode Ren Emrath. Even at this distance Luke was certain of the Box M owner's identity.

Emrath strode across the bare yard with a decided swagger, his dark shirt and pants clean-looking in comparison to his companion's dusty clothes. For a space of a minute the two stood talking. Then the little man mounted, wheeled the chestnut around, and was gone down the trail, riding fast.

Something strikingly familiar about the little man struck Luke again. Suddenly he turned back to his horse and swung into the saddle. There were two hours left until sundown. In those two hours he would find out what had brought Emrath's rider in and out in such haste

He rode up and over the crest of the hill, skirted another, and made a wide circle around the Box M, until he came to the trail that led south. There he had little difficulty in picking up the tracks of the chestnut. He put his gelding into a swinging run and followed.

V

Luke admitted to himself within the next half hour that he had been fortunate in picking this gelding when he made his escape from the jail. The animal had a stamina and speed that closely approached that of his own sorrel.

He reined in occasionally, stopping to listen. But he saw the rider on the chestnut before he heard him. He had followed the other's sign better than five miles, when the rider ahead was skylined for a brief instant as he rode over high ground. From then on it was a matter of drawing up within sight of his quarry and making certain that there was cover ahead before he proceeded.

This became more difficult as he rode on. The hills fell away and ahead stretched a limitless expanse of bunch grass range broken only by an occasional outcropping. Far ahead was the looming rocky mass of Twin Tent Butte. McVickers fell behind, fearing that he might be discovered, following that dust plume hanging to the man's trail. In the slanting rays of the lowering sun that white tracer formed a clear, straight line toward Twin Tent Butte.

Riding in toward the butte, McVickers took a chance and drew up on the other, closely enough so that he could see him again. When the man ahead drew rein at the foot of the piñon-dotted rock slope and dismounted, Luke cut to the right of the other's trail and rode down into a shallow coulée. There he left the saddle, climbed up to where he could get a good view ahead, and waited.

For a full minute Luke lost sight of the rider, then he saw him again, far up among the rocks, climbing upward, working around toward the south face. The man's actions were puzzling. After he had disappeared toward the front of the butte, Luke glanced off to the west, saw the ribbon of trail that came toward the butte. He was about to swing his gaze back to Twin Tent again when he saw, far out along that trail, a hazy blur of dust. Someone was coming, heading in toward Red Dog. Then, unexpectedly, he saw the plan of the man he had followed.

Luke ran down to the gelding, vaulted to the saddle, and rode up out of the coulée. But instead of spurring ahead, he held the animal to a fast walk, reining him carefully to avoid the stretches where the thin soil laid bare the rock, making as little noise as possible.

It took Luke seven minutes to reach the base of the huge outcropping. He rode in close, ground-haltered the gelding, and started the climb upward.

The pain in his shoulder returned, but he disregarded it. His memory brought back thoughts of the many times he had climbed to the top of this butte in his younger days.

He remembered, too, the broad ledge that overhung the trail on the south face. Playing the hunch that he would find the man he followed on that ledge, he worked to a level above it, and only then started around toward it. Below him, the ground fell away until he stared dizzily off over a sheer seventy-foot drop.

A mile out on the trail he clearly made out a buckboard coming toward him. The horses were moving at a fast trot. He took the time to remove his boots, wasting precious seconds in making certain that he could move noiselessly. The buckboard drew closer and with a sudden horror he recognized the two figures on the seat — Judith Walton and Fat Holden.

Behind them, in the wagon, lay a blanket-shrouded object. Instinctively Luke knew that it was Fred Walton's body. Judith was taking her father into town for burial in the cemetery.

He waved desperately, but they came on. They rode, looking neither to left nor right. Although he could not see their faces, he knew that they were so absorbed in the tragedy that had entered their lives that there was little hope of their seeing his signal.

He hurried on, tearing his Levi's on the

sharp rocks, bruising his feet and hands. The approach of the buckboard fascinated him, as he realized how powerless he was to stop it. He saw it come within rifle range, and from then on a feeling of utter helplessness took hold of him.

Abruptly he recognized a familiar stunted piñon that grew out of a crevice in the stratified rock. He looked down and to the left. There, belly down on the wide ledge ten feet below him, a man was looking over the sights of a Winchester trained on the buckboard below. Instant recognition came. He shouted, whipping up his guns: "Tade?"

Tade Barlow's head jerked up. His amazed stare held for a brief second. All at once the gray eyes squinted; he rolled over quickly and clawed at the .45 on his thigh. He cleared it of leather, swung it up. . . .

A blasting, clattering death came down at the killer from above. Five slugs tore into him, beating his head back. The leering, terror-stricken face of the man became a mass of bloody pulp in those two seconds. All five slugs had centered in it.

From below a hoarse cry issued up, and Luke McVickers saw Fat Holden climbing from the buckboard. He waved once, then sat down, gone suddenly weak. He felt his body bathed in a perspiration that the chill of the air made clammy.

"Luke, what is it?" Judith called up as she recognized him.

"Send Holden up here!" was the answer he shouted back before he lay face down, exhausted.

Ten minutes later, Fat Holden climbed into view, a .45 in his hand. He stood twenty feet away, clinging grimly to the rock face, his weapon lined at Luke who was seated on the ledge beside Tade Barlow's body.

"Come on, Fat. I won't bite."

"Unbuckle your hardware first," was Holden's rejoinder.

Luke wearily followed the other's order; only then did Holden come down to stand on the ledge beside him. He looked at the dead gunman and his face lost color.

"Barlow?" he asked.

Luke nodded, and pointed to the rifle.

"I found him up here, lookin' down at you over the sights of that Thirty-Thirty."

Amazement softened the hard lines on Holden's face. "What were you doin' with him?"

"An hour ago he left Emrath at the Box M. I followed him."

Holden's jaw muscles tightened and he gave Luke a long look. "Are you runnin' another sandy?"

Luke sighed. "You can follow the sign straight back to the Box M," he answered.

There was a long moment of silence. Holden looked down guiltily to discover that he still held the .45 in his hand. He dropped it into the holster.

"I never did trust that little sidewinder!" he said savagely. He hesitated, then added: "The way the cards lay now, Luke, Judith and me have a heap of things to take back." Luke made no answer, so Holden went on: "It's clear now . . . that is, what's been happenin' here. Tade dynamited the water hole on Emrath's orders and shot that bronc' of ours himself, leavin' it there so's we'd be blamed."

"Yesterday afternoon Ren Emrath offered me a thousand in gold to dry-gulch Fred Walton," Luke told him. "An' he put another thousand on your hide. I kicked him down the stairs of the Mile High."

"I heard about that," Holden said guiltily. "That was another of those damned things I been huntin' the answer to." He walked over to the edge of the ledge and waved down to Judith, shouting: "We'll be right down!"

Luke rose stiffly to his feet, jerked his head in the direction of the buckboard, and asked: "What's goin' to happen to her, Fat?"

"No tellin'," Holden answered glumly, then added: "I reckon you ought to know what Judith told me this mornin', Luke. It was after you broke jail. She said she didn't think you had a hand in any of this, and she hoped you'd get away."

"That's somethin'," was Luke's dry retort.

Holden shrugged and looked down at Barlow's body once more. "Let's leave this buzzard meat up here where the birds can have easy pickin's."

"Then what?" said Luke.

"You mean you don't know?"

"It might not hurt to ride over to the Box M and see Emrath," was Luke's reply.

Holden nodded grimly. "We'll take Fred into town first. We can't let Judith make the drive alone."

He led the way back down through the rocks. Luke recovered his boots and got the two horses, his own and Barlow's, and rode around to the buckboard.

Judith was standing beside it, talking to Holden as he came up. She looked at Luke and what he saw in her eyes was strangely disquieting.

"It's too late to say it, Luke, but I'm sorry."

Luke nodded toward the buckboard. "I reckon I've made a few bad guesses myself."

Judith all at once examined him more closely, seeing his bandaged shoulder in the fading light. "You're hurt, Luke. How did it happen?"

He chuckled dryly. "It was tagged Circle W. Got it this mornin' right after I excused myself at the lockup. It's nothin'."

VI

They made the three-mile ride in a deep silence. There were things that each one of them would have said, yet they realized the futility of words. At the edge of town the cobalt blanket of a starry night settled down quickly, and ahead the lights of Red Dog winked out. Holden stopped and pointed over to a corral that stood back from the road.

"Your sorrel's over there, Luke. I hid your saddle in that feed bin out behind. Wait here. I'll be back *pronto*."

"What are you two going to do?" Judith asked in alarm.

Luke was glad when Holden drove on without asking him to help explain to her. He turned the two horses into the corral and carried the saddles back to the big empty feed bin. As he lifted his own saddle out of the box, he heard the rapid approach of riders coming along the road. Not wanting to be seen, he hid behind the bin until they had ridden past and on into town. Then he set about snaking out his sorrel.

In less than five minutes he heard running footsteps and made out Holden's gaunt outline in the half light, coming toward him. Holden waited until he caught his breath before he broke the news.

"Ren Emrath just rode in."

Luke suddenly went cold, feeling a clear hatred well up within him. He stepped over to loosen the saddle cinch and without a word led the sorrel back into the corral.

"Well, what are we waitin' on, Fat?" he said then.

Holden fell in step beside him, and they started up the street.

"Where is he?"

"In the Glory Hole. All his crew with him."

They trudged on in silence, Holden forging ahead, until Luke cautioned him: "Take it slower, fat man. We've got the rest of the night for this."

That bantering word seemed to settle things between them. Whatever lay behind was finished now. They were together, ready to take anything that came their way, ready to meet it with smoking guns. Holden's face broke into an open smile.

It was like Holden to push his way through the swing doors of the Hole without once looking in to see what he would be facing. Luke put out a hand to stop him, but he was too late. In one stride he was at his friend's side. His gaze ran over the room. To his right he caught the fat bartender's shifty glance toward a door at the back of the room as the man recognized Holden.

The five men standing at the bar, Box M hands, turned slowly to face them and an absolute silence settled down. A faro dealer and the three men at his table all rose from their chairs.

"Where's Ren Emrath?" Holden's deep voice boomed the question. Not a man made answer.

"Let's try that back room, Fat. Cut down on the first gent that makes a move."

As he spoke, McVickers stepped forward, hands hanging loosely at his sides, fingers bent a little claw-like.

"That place back there's empty." This from the bartender in a hushed voice.

"If you're wrong, I'll be back to see you later," Luke answered, not slowing his pace. The barkeep swallowed.

Past the bar, Luke turned slowly to the others within his vision. Holden had covered him this far, and he waited until Fat joined him, watching to see that no man made a move. Three strides away were the closed double doors to the back room. Already he could hear the murmur of voices coming from it.

He crossed to the doors, thumbed out the butts of his Colts, and breathed: "Keep me covered, Fat." Then, before Holden could answer, he kicked the door open.

In a tent of light from one hanging lamp in the smoke-filled room, five men sat around a poker table. The dealer, Ren Emrath, faced the door and was in the act of filling in one player's hand with two cards. He stiffened in surprise, and the two cards fluttered down from his outstretched hand. Every man at the table turned slowly to face Luke.

He stepped through the doors, swung them completely open until they thudded back against the thin partition. "Which one o' you is first?" he drawled.

He watched closely, picking instinctively the thin-faced little man with the gray eyes, sitting at Emrath's right. The man came up out of his chair, his lips drawing down into a sneer.

"An even break. Why not?" he growled, and moved as he spoke.

Before the little gunman's hand had

179

reached his weapon, Luke's two .38's flashed up swiftly in a motion that was sheer magic. He stood rock-steady for the fraction of a second, then squeezed the triggers. The thundering roar marked a blue hole that centered on the gray-eyed man's forehead. He sprawled forward across the table without a sound. The others remained frozen in their chairs.

Emrath stared dumbly at the dead man one instant and looked back at Luke the next. "What the hell are you doin', McVickers?" he said evenly.

"Tade Barlow talked," Luke lied, and waited.

Ren Emrath swallowed with difficulty. "I don't know what you mean. See here, McVickers, if you think. . . ."

"I caught him up in the rocks at Twin Tent," Luke interrupted. "He lived long enough to tell me that he had put the dynamite up in Jackson's Draw at your orders." It was a wild guess but he knew from Emrath's expression that he had hit the mark. "He laid two killin's onto you, Emrath, Walton's and . . . Jeff McVickers's."

He tensed at the change in Emrath's expression. What he saw set up a quiet fury within him. Slowly he lowered his guns and dropped them back into holsters.

"Because you waited a year to buy the Box M from the bank, you thought no one would ever find you out." He waited a moment during which the silence palled on them, then he added: "You can make your play any time now."

Emrath's glance shifted down from Luke's face to his guns, then back again. He got up from his chair, moving slowly, keeping his hands, palms down, on the green felt padding of the table.

Once erect, the arrogant bearing Luke so well remembered returned. Emrath jerked his head, indicating the dead man.

"Bill, here, was always a little slow gettin' his hardware out. I'm not. You made your mistake when you let me get on my feet, McVickers."

With a hurried nervousness Emrath flashed his hand to the .45 at his thigh.

They moved together. Luke was calm now, putting all the old precision in that one swift lightning play of muscle. As his palm slapped the gun butt and flicked it upward, Emrath's three remaining companions were already leaping from their chairs. He forgot them as his .38 roared and found its mark.

Fear dilated to brief bewilderment in Emrath's eyes; he was trying to complete the upward swing of his six-gun when life left him.

The force of the shot toppled him over backward. Luke lunged sideways, swung his weapon briefly to the side to cover the mustached man there who was swinging up his six-gun. He lanced out another shot, saw the other's weapon fly from his grasp, and then he whirled.

The move saved his life and the slug intended for his heart was like a hot iron running along his ribs at his side. Once more he snapped his .38 around and threw a shot; the man who had hit him screamed horribly, clawed his chest, and staggered to the wall to lean against it with staring, death-ridden eyes.

Above the splitting crash of sound in the room, Luke heard the staccato crash of shots behind him. Holden had opened up. The next instant the two men who faced him threw down their guns. He leaned over to catch hold of the door, and then sprang backward through it, slamming it shut after him.

When he faced about, he saw Holden's gun stabbing at a man who stood at the faro table. The gunman let his six-shooter fall, looked down in horror at a spot of red rapidly spreading across his shirt front, and then sank to his knees to fall heavily forward.

Holden looked about, and lowered his .45. "It don't look like anyone else wants to buy into this game."

Luke's reply was cut off by the sight of Sheriff Len Thomas striding through the swing doors at the front. He held a .45 in his hand, but, when he looked about to find that only Holden and McVickers were there, he dropped it in his holster. And as he stepped forward toward them, Luke saw that Judith was standing behind the lawman. Their glances met and held and he read the horror in her eyes.

Holden was saying: "You'd better take a look in that back room, Len. It may need cleanin' up a bit."

Luke forced his gaze to break with Judith's, and followed the sheriff back. When the doors had been kicked open, they felt the icy breeze that blew through the open window. The three dead men lay where they had fallen, Emrath behind the table.

Thomas took one look down at him, paled slightly, and growled: "He had us fooled plenty." Looking at Luke, he added: "Judith told me all about it. Did you learn anything more?"

"He killed Fred Walton and my father."

For a moment there was an awkward silence. Behind him Luke heard a soft step and knew without turning that Judith Walton was standing there

Then she was speaking, her voice low and throaty with emotion: "We owe you so much, Luke. If you and I could only go back seven years. . . ."

Luke faced her bewilderedly, a wild joy choking back the things he would have said. She read his look, and took the step that put her in his arms.

Holden coughed nervously and jerked his head irritably at Len Thomas. The two of them went out quietly, as though a noise might have disturbed the two they left there. . . .

THREE-CORNERED WAR

Titling this story "Three-Cornered War," Jon Glidden sent it on to his agent in early March, 1937. She sent it on to Popular Publications where Rogers Terrill, who edited *Dime Western,* read it and suggested some changes. These the author made and the story was returned to Terrill on April 14, 1937. Terrill bought it on May 22, 1937. The author was paid $101.70. It appeared in *Dime Western* (8/37) under the title "Yuma Sends Back a Man!" The author's title and revised manuscript have been followed for its appearance here.

I

After you've been up thirty-six hours helping at the birth of a future cowpuncher of San Dimas County, you can't think very fast. I couldn't, anyway. That's why I didn't get what Soapy Rains was trying to tell me from across my plate of ham and eggs that morning.

He had to say it again before I got it. And when I did, I forgot that I'd been half starved for the past two days, and forgot about the ham and eggs that were sitting right there, hot and waiting, on my plate.

"Well, Doc, the Three-Cornered War is in town today."

"You mean Lew King rode in?"

Soapy nodded. "It's his first time on a Saturday."

He knew as well as I did that Lew King shouldn't be in town on a busy day. For the five months since Lew had been paroled from Yuma, he'd kept pretty much to himself. He wasn't supposed to carry guns for a year, and he wasn't giving himself the chance of wanting to carry them. At least, up to today.

"Bud Pierce drove his buckboard in half an hour ago," Soapy went on. "Laura was with him. I wonder if they see each other any more?"

"Laura and Lew King? No, I don't reckon they do."

"Bud was a damned fool to do what he did," Soapy growled. "In threatenin' to shoot Lew if he ever caught him with his sister again, he drove her straight to Mel Brand."

"He didn't drive her," I said. "Laura probably loves Mel."

"The hell she does!" he exploded. "That girl's still in love with Lew, and you know it. She had two reasons for gettin' engaged to Mel Brand. In the first place, she wanted to ease things and show Bud she was through with Lew. And in the second, Mel's bank holds the mortgage on the Pierce outfit . . . a mortgage that won't be paid unless she marries Mel."

"You're runnin' off at the mouth, Soapy."

Soapy snorted. "And who cares if I do? You and a lot of others know that Lew King never rustled them steers of Pierce's five years ago. And Laura knows he didn't. But Bud wants to be stubborn, saying that the loss of that herd killed their father and that Lew's to blame. And because of him bein' so hog-headed, Laura will marry Mel."

"Maybe you'd think the same if you were Bud," I said.

"No, I wouldn't, Doc," he said seriously. "But if I did, I'd want more proof than Bud's got." He paused for a long moment, staring out his front window. Finally he turned back to me, and said: "I wonder if Bud or Laura will bump into Lew today?"

Soapy called the turn that morning. It happened just as I was leaving his place and

187

walking up toward Mel Brand's bank, which sits on one of the four corners of Pima's only cross streets. I saw Lew King coming down the walk toward me, his flat, big frame moving with an ease that always made people look at him twice. He spotted me and grinned.

"Doc, you're the man I'm lookin' for. One of my new calves is down sick with the fever. I want you to ride out and have a look at him."

"What's the matter with George Ernst?" I asked. "I've got enough to do with all this grippe around town. I'm no cow nurse."

He just stood there and smiled, and, as usual, we understood each other without having to waste words. George Ernst had taken his veterinary learning at a meat-packing house in Kansas City, someone once said. It was true, too, so far as any of us knew.

"I need some sleep," I told him finally. "I'll ride out late this afternoon."

All at once I saw his glance go beyond me, and, with the shifting of his gray eyes, his lean face sobered instantly. It hardened, like I remembered seeing it that time when he'd stood trial, five years back.

"I'll be waitin' for you, Doc," he said without any hurry. Then he turned and started off up the walk.

Behind me, I heard Bud Pierce say: "Not so fast, King. I want to see you."

Pierce walked on past me, with his big frame almost as tall as Lew's and looking a good bit heavier.

"Howdy, Bud," Lew drawled, as he stopped and faced around.

"I've told Laura I'll horse whip her the next time she rides over to see you, King," Bud said, not wasting words. "The same things goes for you. Stay away from her."

"Laura's bronc' had a stone in his hoof the other day," Lew said evenly. "Could I help it if she rode in at my place and asked me to take the stone out for her?"

This, from Lew King, was as surprising to me as a delivery of triplets. It was plenty plain right then that Lew, for once, was swallowing his pride to keep trouble from breaking out. Later, I was to remember it.

But Bud Pierce wouldn't have it that way; he was feeling ornery, and meant to make the best of this opportunity. "And stay outside our fences, Lew," he said. "Thirty head of beef strayed out of our upper pasture this week."

That was the thing that did it. It was dynamite to say that, and Bud must have known it. Lew King's lean face lost a little of its tan. I saw him suddenly turn rigid, and the next thing I saw was a blur as his right fist was swung.

Bud weaved out of the way and stepped back. His face was set in a taut smile as he reached around to unbuckle his belt and drop his holstered .45 on the boardwalk. I heard him say: "Just in case I lose my head, Lew."

He swung as he spoke, and every ounce of his 180 pounds was behind that blow. It caught Lew King fully in the chest, driving him back against the adobe wall of the bank. Lew lost his footing and sprawled to the boards, looking ridiculous and hurt. It did hurt, too, but hurt his pride worse than anything else. He lunged to his feet and stepped in, driving his fists at Bud Pierce so fast that my eyes couldn't follow the blows.

The tables turned right then. One of his punches caught Bud alongside the head and seemed to loose all the unreasoning anger in the man. Bud went wild, and Lew, seeing it, fought warily. He didn't rush in like Bud was doing, but kept out of the way, lashing in now and then like a striking rattler.

The crowd gathered quickly. Once, when Bud was down for a couple of seconds, I took my eyes off them long enough to look across and see Mel Brand standing in the crowd at the foot of the steps to the bank. Mel's outfit was different than the rest. He wore a black coat and a white shirt and string tie, as a banker should. He was dark-haired, his eyes coal-black, and he wasn't so tanned as the rest. He'd have stood out among any crowd.

Looking back again, I was nearly too late to miss the end of the scrap. Bud crouched where he'd fallen for maybe two seconds, and then he lunged. He wasn't trying to hit Lew; he was trying to get his arms around him so that he could break his back. Lew shot out a stiff right, and Bud dodged — dodged right into a left that was packed with more dynamite than I've ever seen in a man's fist. It caught Bud on the point of the jaw and loosened him at the knees so that he kept right on coming, only falling to his knees, and then straightening out, flat on his face, unmoving.

Lew was breathing heavily; he planted his feet apart and stood there looking down at Bud with all the hardness gone out of his eyes and a hurt look in its place. I realized then that he was sorry for what had happened.

Mel Brand stepped out of the crowd and came over to kneel beside Bud. Mel lifted his head and saw the blood running out of his mouth. He got up then and said: "Get some water and a towel." Then he faced Lew. "I wish to God you had the guts to pack a gun, King," he snarled.

Lew, jerking his head around at the words, stepped over to Mel. He planted one fist on Mel's white shirt front and twisted the shirt. He struck Mel an open-handed wallop that rattled his teeth.

"Take that back, Mel," he drawled. "Either that, or shed your hardware and have more of the same."

Mel's face twisted into an ugly grimace. If a man ever had hate showing in his eyes, Mel Brand had it then. He knew he'd said something he couldn't back — something that wasn't fair — but he wasn't reasoning then.

With a sudden gesture, he swept his coat back and reached for the ivory-handled .45 he carried in a black leather holster hanging at his belt. His hand never reached the butt of that gun. Lew's fist darted down and flicked the six-shooter out and into the dust of the street. I reached out just as Lew was cocking his arm, ready to hit Mel squarely in the face.

"Take it easy, Lew!" I yelled. I was almost as young as Lew, a little heavier maybe, and pretty strong, but I had all I could do to hold back that arm.

Then, as suddenly as it had taken hold of him, all the anger went out of Lew King. He shoved Mel away from him, and turned to me and said: "Get me out of this, Doc."

He let me lead him out through the crowd. He was rubbing his left hand as we walked away, and his lips were clamped tightly shut with pain; he'd hurt his hand in hitting Bud Pierce that last blow.

"Better come up to the office and let me fix it," I growled. I wasn't so pleased at having taken a part in what had happened. It didn't do to choose sides in a thing like this.

Right then I saw Tom Nelson crossing the street toward the crowd, and I turned out to stop him. Nelson was Pima's lawman in those days, and a good one. He was the one who'd arrested Lew and locked him up five years ago — which was the one act of his life he regretted. For Tom, like a few of us others, decided later that Lew had been framed.

"No use going over, Tom," I told him. "I can tell you all about it."

I did, too, wanting to be sure that he got a straight story. When I'd finished, he looked across at Lew King and walked over to where Lew stood waiting for me.

Tom shook his head and said: "You had a

right to do it, Lew, but you've bought into something that'll be hard to finish."

"It wasn't Lew's fault," I protested. "I tell you, Bud. . . ."

"Lew knows what I mean," Tom interrupted. Then, seeing that a few of the more curious were drifting along the walk toward us, Tom led us down to his office at the jail.

"You shouldn't have come in today," the lawman said, after he'd closed the door and crossed over to sit in his battered swivel chair at the desk.

"I had to," Lew explained. "I forgot the date. I missed reportin' on the Fifteenth."

"Hell!" Tom flared. "I don't give one damn about your reportin'! If the parole board knew you half as well as I do, they wouldn't ask it."

That was the first I'd ever heard of Lew King's having to report to the sheriff. Later, I learned that Lew had done it religiously twice a month.

"The smart thing to do would be for you to climb your saddle and head for home," Tom went on. "And forget about this, Lew. I'll have a talk with Mel and Bud and tell them to take it easy."

"I don't need your help," Lew said flatly.

Tom sat there, reaching up to tap his badge with a blunt forefinger, saying: "No, I reckon you don't. But it's my job to keep you out of trouble for six months longer. After that, I'm givin' you your guns out of the safe and puttin' on a pair of blinders. Then, if you go skunk huntin', it won't be my look-out."

That was a long speech for Tom Nelson; it was also the first time I'd ever heard him say anything against Mel Brand. For, indirect as his words had been, I knew he was referring to Mel. I suppose he felt the same way as I did about Mel and Laura.

Lew crossed to the door, opened it, and said: "I'd like to ride over to Benson one day next week. There's a gent over there wantin' to sell some feeders."

"Hell, go ahead!" Tom exploded. "And no more reportin'! The parole board be damned! You stay away from town for a while."

When Lew was gone, Tom spent five minutes striding up and down his office, cursing and lighting into Mel Brand for what he'd said. "That's Mel's way," he growled. "He knows as well as I do that Lew can't carry an iron."

Later, I was sitting in the chair at the sheriff's front window, where I could keep an eye on the stairs leading up to my office. I had two rooms in the second story of the building next to the bank, and the steps to it climbed up between the two buildings. I saw Laura Pierce come up the street, look up at my window, and start climbing the stairs. So I told Tom I had work to do, and left his office.

Laura met me, coming down again after not finding me in. Neither of us said a word. She turned and led the way back up and didn't speak until the door to my waiting room was closed. Then she turned to me. "Why did you let it happen, Fred?"

Laura Pierce was one of the few people who ever called me by name in those days, and I suppose that it gave me another reason for liking her. Once, years back, before Lew came to our range, I'd been in love with her. Perhaps I still was — yes, I know I was — but it was more like being her brother since I'd found how she felt about Lew.

Just now her hazel eyes were brighter than usual, and the long ride into town had whipped her chestnut hair so that it now caught the light and shone like spun red gold. She was never more beautiful than at times like this when an inner fire took hold of her and heightened her olive coloring.

"How could I stop it?" I asked, a little lamely, for she had reminded me that I might have done something.

She sat down all at once in one of my rickety straight-backed chairs, and buried her face in her hands and murmured: "I still love him, Fred. I love him."

When she looked up at me again, unashamed, all I could do was nod and say: "Bud said you saw Lew out at his place."

"It was the first time," she told me, half-way defending herself. "I hadn't known how much he means to me. He's big and fine and honest . . . and he loves me."

"He didn't tell you so?"

"No." She shook her head. "But I saw it in his eyes, Fred. I'll always see it, every time we meet. How can I go through with it?" she asked helplessly. She sat there silently for a moment, with a stricken look haunting her regular features, and her eyes finally lighting up in anger as she added: "And to think that Mel would throw it up to him that way."

"Forget it," I told her. "Mel was sore, and so was Lew. It'll blow over."

"Not with Mel," she said, her voice almost a whisper. "He'll never be satisfied until he's even with Lew. He's . . . he's cruel, Fred. I don't love him. I never will, now."

"Then you know what to do." The words were out before I thought, and I realized that they had pulled me deeper into this whole thing than I wanted to be. Long ago I'd decided to stay clear of it, that nothing I could do would help Laura Pierce.

She was sitting there, pondering what I'd said, when we both heard the heavy tread of boots on the stairs outside.

She got up out of her chair, saying — "I'll go now." — when the door swung open on Bud Pierce.

He held a bloody bandanna over his hurt mouth, and his brown eyes shuttled between the two of us as he came in and closed the door.

Laura's face lost color and her eyes flashed again in that quick anger. "I hope you're really hurt," she breathed.

Strangely enough, Bud Pierce hung his head and answered: "Go ahead. I've got it comin'."

II

It hit us both between the eyes, Laura and me. Here was Bud Pierce, stubborn and willful and as bull-headed as any man who ever drew breath, admitting he was in the wrong.

Laura broke the awkward silence; she rushed over to her brother, threw her arms around him, and cried: "You mean that,

Bud? You know it wasn't Lew's fault?"

He nodded, taking her arms gently and pushing her away, as though disgusted with himself. He was, too, as his next words proved, for he looked down at her and said: "I'm taking back everything I ever said against Lew King, Sis."

"But . . . but why, Bud?" Laura gasped.

He smiled mysteriously and told us: "I think I've found the answer. You heard me say this mornin' that some critters were missin' from one of our herds, Doc? Laura knows I've been thinkin' Lew took those steers. Well, I took the trouble to follow their sign and see where they went. I lost 'em the same place we lost that herd five years ago . . . down in the brakes below Mission Springs."

He hesitated a long moment, as if halfway looking for me to say something. But now wasn't the time for me to talk, so I waited.

He went on: "I found something. It was the same this time as before. Whoever drove off the critters wrapped the hoofs of his bronc' with burlap, so that the sign wouldn't show. This time only one man did the rustlin'. And he got careless. He took the wrappings off his bronc's shoes too soon. I saw his sign, and I'd know it if I saw it again. The back quarter of the right front shoe was broken off."

Again he paused, so this time I put in: "It would be easy to check Lew King on that, Bud."

He nodded. "I know. And I did check it. It took me all day yesterday, hidin' up on the ridge above his layout until he rode away. That's how I knew you'd seen him, Sis," he explained, turning to Laura. "Thinkin' what I did, it riled me to see you ride in there and talk to him."

"What did you find out, Bud?" she asked breathlessly.

"When he rode away, I went down and looked at the shoes of every bronc' in his corral. It wasn't one of those. So I'd seen all but the one he was ridin', and it was too grassy around there to read that. If I'd taken the trouble to go to the livery stable before I met Lew this mornin', this wouldn't have happened. It wasn't him. I've been to every blacksmith in town. He hasn't had a shoe changed in a month. So I'm here to eat my words, Doc, and say that I don't think it was Lew who stole my stock five years ago."

"But who . . . ?" Laura began.

Bud cut her off: "I don't know, but I'm ready to make my peace with Lew."

"He's gone," I told him. "He rode out of town to keep out of your way."

200

"Then I'll ride over to see him tonight after we get home."

Up until now I'd disliked Bud Pierce, even hated him. But now it came to me that Bud was all man, for it took a real man to stand there and say the things he'd just said.

He wasn't through with his surprises, either, for a moment later he turned to Laura: "I heard about what Mel said to Lew, Sis. It was a polecat trick."

Never before had I seen Laura's eyes light up the way they did then. Happiness radiated from her face. Bud caught it, the same as I did, and added: "As far as I'm concerned, you're not marryin' Mel, Laura."

She was in his arms then, choking back the tears as she kissed his swollen lips. I left them alone, going into my office and spending five minutes feeling relieved and sorting out the extra instruments I'd packed away in my case the afternoon before. Just as I was finishing, Bud came into the office, alone.

"You've got to do something to this cut on my lip, Doc," he said. "Lew damn' near ripped it off."

The cut wasn't as bad as he'd made out, and I knew he had another reason for having stayed to see me. After I'd finished, his reason came out.

"I'm goin' to make the break with Mel this afternoon, Doc," he told me. "If anything should happen, I want you to look after Laura and Lew."

"What the hell could happen?" I asked bluntly, not wanting to be any more involved in this than I was. I'd forgotten about the mortgage the bank held — and forgotten what it would mean if Laura didn't marry Mel Brand. It might mean the loss of the outfit for Bud and Laura, since Bud Pierce hadn't inherited his father's money-making ability.

Bud shook his head at my question. "I don't know, Doc," he murmured. "Some queer things have happened lately. Three nights ago, someone took a shot at me as I was ridin' up to one of our line shacks. I haven't told Laura."

In one small instant I felt the weight settle back on my shoulders — the weight that had been lifted a few minutes ago when I realized that Lew King and Laura were now free to have each other.

"You're seein' spooks, Bud," I said, trying to make my voice lighter than what I felt down inside me.

"No, it's not spooks. But if it isn't Lew, who is it?"

I couldn't answer that any better than he

could. We sat there for a few moments longer, and then Bud got up out of his chair and put his broad-brimmed Stetson back on again and opened the door.

"Be seein' you around, Doc," was all he said as he left.

I was busy all that day. First, it was two more cases of grippe down in the Mexican settlement at the east end of town, and then Harry Bain brought in one of his riders with a broken leg that had to be set. It was while I was bandaging that leg, shortly before four in the afternoon, that I happened to look out my window and saw Bud and Laura heading out of town in the buckboard.

Because I was so busy, and because I needed sleep, I'd completely forgotten about riding out to Lew King's to look at his sick calf. Later, I remembered it, and knew he wouldn't mind because of its being Saturday and a busy day with me.

Usually I'd have quite a few patients Saturday nights, and occasionally an honest soul who came in to pay up what he owed me. This particular night, collections weren't so good, or patients, either, for that matter. In fact, shortly after seven, with no one in the office, I stretched out on the office couch hoping to get a little sleep. It wasn't but a few minutes before I heard the door behind me squeak open. I looked up to see Lew King standing there.

He held out his left hand and I could see that it was swollen and red. "You'd better do something to this, Doc," he drawled. "It slipped my mind this mornin'."

As I set to work at the hand, I looked at him to see if he'd heard the news. He hadn't, or his eyes wouldn't have had that hard glitter.

"Did you run into Bud Pierce?" I asked finally.

He smiled wryly. "I came in steppin' mighty careful, Doc. Left my bronc' down in the back alley. No one's gettin' the chance to say I'm lookin' for trouble."

I didn't tell him about the news of Bud's discovery, thinking how much better it would be for him to get it firsthand from Bud. Probably I wouldn't have had the chance, anyway, for inside of five minutes three patients were waiting out front to see me.

I bandaged Lew's hand with its broken bone as well as I could, gave him some liniment, and told him to ride straight home and get it into some hot water. He left, going out the side office door that leads into the hall, so he wouldn't have to meet the people in the waiting room.

It was ten minutes after eight when I heard the shouting down on the street. As soon as I'd cleared the office, I went down. It was too late.

Larry Shumway, at the livery barn, told me what had happened.

"All hell's cut loose, Doc!" he said, excitedly. "Pitcher Wade rode in a few minutes ago on that bronc' you hear wheezin' back there in that stall. He rode straight in from the fork in the Bitter Creek trail that cuts off up to Lew King's. Guess what he found lyin' there at the fork?"

He paused, so I said: "Let's have it, Larry."

"He found Bud Pierce. Shot three times through the back. Dead!"

I leaned up against the frame siding alongside the door; I had to, feeling a slow weakness settle through me at the shock.

"What's the matter, Doc?" Larry asked, frowning and looking at me.

"Go on. What happened?" I snapped at him.

"Tom Nelson got up a posse and headed out for Lew's place not five minutes ago."

"They're after Lew?"

He nodded.

Larry Shumway's a talker and would have told me more. But just then a couple others came up and he started telling them about it, and I had the chance to slip away unnoticed.

If there was anything I could have done — if I could have saddled up and ridden out to warn Lew — I'd have done it. But I couldn't hope to start out behind the posse, circle it, and get to Lew's layout in time to warn him. *Besides,* I thought, as I crossed over to O'Reilley's Bar, *Tom Nelson won't lose his head.*

I had four straight shots of whiskey at O'Reilley's, standing alone at the end of his bar and doing my best to quiet those who were already talking a necktie party. There wasn't much I had to go on yet, except that I knew Lew hadn't done it. What worried me most was to see Mel Brand come in and start spending his money like water.

He was smooth about it, too, not saying anything openly against Lew but buying drinks for any man who would take them. In the hour I stood there, Mel changed that crowd from an excited and angry bunch of men into a raging, blood-hungry mob — a mob drunk on the whiskey he'd paid for and drunk with a frenzy for vengeance.

It was a good thing I moved out when I did, around 10:30. Not five minutes after I'd gone up to my office to get my old Colt

.45, I had the chance to use it. Tom Nelson and his posse rode into town with Lew King, and they had a hard time making the jail.

My lining up behind Tom with my six-shooter in my fist to hold the crowd back may have done some good. It did, at least with a few of the more sober ones, for one of them stepped out and shouted, above the roar of voices:

"Stand back, gents! Doc Tupper'll see we get a square deal!"

That helped — just long enough to let Tom unlock his door and shove Lew inside. In another minute he was back again with his sawed-off shotgun hugged to his flat belly. Seeing that, those closest quieted instantly, passing the word back so that a lowering silence crept out across the street. Those nearest moved back a little, so that we stood there with our guns leveled and ringed by a solid semicircle of faces.

"Clear out!" Tom shouted, a little louder than was necessary now. "Have you all gone loco?"

"We're here to hang King!" someone yelled in a whiskey-thick voice. A few shouts from the outer fringes of the crowd greeted these words, but the rest were quiet, seeing the expression on Tom Nelson's face.

"For eleven years I've toted this badge without gettin' it slimed up," Tom told them. "If Lew King gets out of this jail tonight, it'll be after you've beefed yourself a sheriff! Now get the hell away from here before I blow someone's guts out!"

Tom never did waste words; he wasn't wasting them now. It may be that a milder man could have held back that mob, but I doubt it. And they moved when he spoke, backing away and off the walk and over across the street and in under the store awnings.

Tom turned to the rest of us, and snapped: "Jerry, you and Frypan get out back. Red and Ollie can stay here in front. Shoot the first blood-yowlin' gent who makes war talk." He examined their faces for a brief instant, adding: "I mean it, too!" Then he turned to me. "Doc, you get in here with me."

Inside, in the unlighted office, we found Lew King standing at one side of the front window, looking out across the street. Tom Nelson reached up and took a lantern down from a peg on the wall, and told us: "C'mon back here with me, you two."

He led us through the side door of the small room and into the cell-block where he lighted the lantern.

He didn't bother locking Lew in a cell. Instead, Lew and I went into one and sat down side-by-side on a cot, and Tom stood at the door, leaning against it and looking down at Lew.

"Now let's have it, Lew," Tom finally said.

But Lew didn't have time to answer. We heard the front office door open, and quick steps crossing the room, and then Tom Nelson was whirling around and drawing his six-gun, lining it at the open doorway.

Laura Pierce stepped through that door, her eyes catching the lantern light so that the tears made them sparkle with unusual brightness.

I felt Lew get up off the cot beside me, and saw Laura hesitate just outside the bars, near where Tom Nelson stood, her glance running on past me and fixing on Lew.

"You . . . it wasn't you, Lew?" she said, her voice low and husky.

"No, it wasn't," he answered simply. And the next instant she had brushed past me and was in Lew's arms, her shoulders moving a little as she let the tears come.

It was like that. Lew's words had carried with her, and she loved him enough to believe what he said, to give herself to him right there before Tom and me. At that moment I don't believe even Tom Nelson was embarrassed; certainly I wasn't — not even when Lew reached down tenderly and tilted her chin up and, looking deeply in her eyes, kissed her.

Laura looked over at Tom then — because he was sheriff, I suppose — and said quietly: "Lew couldn't have done this, Tom. He had no quarrel with Bud."

It wasn't only Tom Nelson's face that took on a look of incredulity; it was Lew King's, too. He took Laura's shoulders and turned her back to face him once more.

"Say that again, Laura," he gasped.

"Then he didn't tell you?" she cried. She shot a look at me. "Fred knows. Don't you, Fred?"

I nodded, and for the next five minutes Laura was telling Tom and Lew the things I already knew — with the exception of what Bud had told me about his being shot at, which was something I had to add. I ended by asking her: "What did Bud do tonight? Was he riding over to see Lew, like he said he would?"

"Yes. We ate late, and Bud saddled up afterward and left the house about six-thirty. He was happier than I've seen him in months." She hid her face in her hands then, not wanting us to see her tears.

"Tom, Lew was in my office right after

seven tonight." I pointed to Lew's bandaged hand. "He didn't leave for nearly half an hour. What time did they find Bud?"

"Around seven," Tom told us, his shaggy brows gathering in a frown that told me he was already seeing what I'd seen minutes ago.

"Then it couldn't have been Lew? Are you sure about the time, Doc?"

"Dead certain," I answered. "Bud was alive at six-thirty, and it would take him at least twenty minutes to ride to where he was found. Lew couldn't have made it in to town from there in less than an hour. He didn't do it. There's your proof."

"Hell, who said I wanted proof?" Tom flared. But then he sighed audibly and his eyes squinted coldly at some inner thought. I read that thought, and so did Lew, I saw, looking over at him.

It may be that Laura Pierce had guessed it, too, although Tom didn't give her time to ask any questions. He took her by the arm, led her out of the cell, and told her: "Get on over to the hotel, Laura. Stay there until I send for you. And don't worry."

Laura looked back once at Lew before she went out. She smiled, and that smile was enough to give any man confidence. Lew visibly straightened when he intercepted it.

211

Tom was back again in less than half a minute. He reached into a back pocket for his keys and said: "Doc, you come out of there. I'm goin' to lock this door. Right now there's things I have to do."

"Such as?" I asked.

"Such as seein' Mel Brand, and askin' him where he was between six and eight tonight."

III

We both watched Tom walk out the door, and I think both of us heard the rattle of his keys as he threw them onto his desk. I know I did, and that it started me thinking.

Finally I turned back to Lew and said: "He'll turn you loose later."

"He'll find that Mel wasn't out of town," he answered.

There was no way of my guessing what made Lew say that. It's what I'd been thinking, though, thinking that Mel Brand would never leave his back trail so open.

"If Mel was in town, it means Tom'll have to keep you locked up here until he finds out who killed Bud," I said, speaking my thoughts aloud. And then, as if to make the words more ominous, we heard noise out on the street again — shouts and cries and unintelligible threats.

"Mel's been buying a lot of free whiskey tonight," I added.

Lew nodded his head, not answering.

I didn't tell Lew what I was doing. I went on into the office and groped around in the dark until I'd located Tom's desk. Then I got the keys. As I came back into the cell-room, Lew saw the keys in my hand. He shook his head "That would be a hell of a trick to pull on Tom Nelson."

"Maybe so," I told him. "But Tom would rather keep you alive than see you swingin' from a cottonwood. You're leavin', Lew."

"Not just yet."

I unlocked the cell door and swung it open. "You're leavin' right now," I said. "I'll stay and take care of Tom. I'll give that mob less'n an hour to work up guts enough to break in here. Hurry it up, Lew."

"To hell with you, Doc," he drawled. "I stick here."

"And Laura," I reminded him. "What about her? Bud told me this mornin' to watch out for the two of you."

He stood there for perhaps five long seconds, looking at me with eyes that I couldn't hope to read. Finally he asked: "How will you make it up to Tom? It'll ruin him."

"Cut out the horseplay, Lew," I said irritably. "Did I ever let you down?"

It was a second or two before he finally said: "You've called the deal. I'll let you play out your hand. How do I get out?"

"Wait here a minute," I told him, and was through the door before he could protest. I went out front and walked up to Red Wilson, one of Tom's posse men, who stood down at the far end of the building. "How does it look, Red?"

"Bad," he said. "Bad." He waved an arm to point across the street. Over there the crowd was lined two deep along the margins of the walk. "Someone's passin' out free drinks."

"It's Mel Brand," I told him. "I'm goin' out back to send the others around here."

In a few brief words I told Frypan Henderson and Jerry Smith what was doing up front, ending by saying: "You'd better get up there with the others until Tom gets back."

Both of them knew me well enough to realize that I was Tom's friend. It wasn't surprising that they accepted my advice and went around to the front of the jail. I left them there with the other two and went back in to Lew again.

He had been thinking it over and changed his mind once more. And again, the only way I could bring him around was by mentioning Laura, and by showing him what a slim chance for his life he had in remaining here. Finally he gave in. We opened the window at the back of the office and he stepped out into the darkness, after I'd handed him my six-shooter.

I stood there listening for a full minute, expecting each second to hear the roar of shots blast out. But they didn't; the only sounds came from the crowd out front. And with the passage of time I felt easier.

At last, I shut the window and crossed the darkened room to sit in Tom Nelson's chair behind his desk. I was sitting there when Tom returned, ten minutes later.

"What about it, Tom?"

He gave a sigh, then answered: "Not a damned thing to help, Doc. Mel worked late in his office. I found two people who saw him. Harvey Thompson, across the street from the bank, claims he saw Mel standing at his window lighting a cigar at seven o'clock. So Mel's story holds water as good as Lew's."

There was a long silence, neither of us speaking. At last, Tom asked: "What would you do, Doc?"

"I've already done it."

"What?"

"Turned Lew loose."

He cursed softly, crossed the room, and stood in the lighted doorway of the cell-block. After he'd looked in, he turned back to me and I could catch a smile on his half-lighted face.

"That's what I was goin' to do, Doc. Now to make it look right, we'll have to tie each other up."

"Not me," I said. "I'm goin' with Lew."

"Where?"

"Into the brakes below Mission Springs."

He nodded, making no protest, saying finally: "Well, let's get this over with. That mob's gettin' ripe for a rush."

In five minutes I had him laced up with his own lariat. I gagged him, leaving the gag as loose as I could and still have it look right. He was lying on the cot where Lew and I had sat earlier. It wasn't very comfortable for him, but we both knew he wouldn't be there long.

I blew out the lantern and took a six-shooter off the rack in the office before I left. Over across the street the crowd was getting up more courage; a few of them were yelling across at the guards, and then I saw a bunch of them spill off the walk and edge out into the street.

"Don't call Tom unless you have to," I told

Frypan Henderson. "He's talkin' to Lew. They may have something."

"It'd better be damned quick," Frypan growled. "We'll be duckin' bullets inside the next half hour."

I walked on down to the livery stable and found Larry Shumway's boy and told him to saddle up my buckskin, that I'd been called out on a case. Then I walked back across the street to the stairs and climbed up to my office.

As the match flared in my hand, I saw an unfamiliar shadow beside one of the front windows. I threw the match to the floor and lunged to one side, and reached for my gun.

A familiar and unwelcome voice spoke out: "It's me, Doc." It was Lew King.

"Why're you here?" I growled irritably. "I told you to fork a bronc' and light out."

The reason I had left instructions to have my horse saddled was that I felt sure Lew would be heading straight for Mission Springs, for out beyond the springs, in the brakes, lay the answer to Bud Pierce's death.

"Come over here, Doc. There's something down here I want you to see."

I crossed and stood alongside him at the window, and looked down to where he was pointing. Below, a few stragglers hurried along the walk, most of them headed up toward the jail where we could hear the murmur of the crowd.

"What is it?" I didn't see anything out of the way.

"The gent standin' in front of the hardware store," Lew said. "Ever see him before?"

I picked out the man he meant, and shook my head.

"It's Flint Harrod. I knew him once in Yuma."

The man stood in the shadow to one side of the dimly lit window of the store opposite. I could see enough of him to get an idea of how he looked; he was small, so slight that the two guns riding low on his thighs looked to be weighing him down. As I looked, he shoved out from the wall and flicked a cigarette into the street, and then eased indolently back again. That one gesture was a pretty fair key to the man; it had been quick and cat-like, yet easy and effortless.

"What about him?" I asked.

"He's a killer," Lew said. "Maybe I'm wrong, but I'm waitin' right here to see what he does."

"Where'll that get you?"

I could see Lew shrug his shoulders. "Maybe nowhere. We'll see."

If I'd pried him with a few more questions, he might have told me what was on his mind right then. But I didn't — I didn't have time to.

"Take a look now," Lew breathed the next instant.

Once more I glanced downward, to see Mel Brand's thick-set figure coming down the walk, the few lights from the store windows sending his elongated shadow streaking out across the dusty, rutted street.

He stopped almost in front of Flint Harrod, only out at the edge of the walk. Then he reached into a pocket for a match, flicked it alight, and held it to the stub of a cigar.

The window was open and I had a good look at Mel. Although the distance was too great to be sure, I could swear that I saw his lips move. A moment later and he was walking back toward the corner. He crossed the street there, coming over to the bank.

"Now watch Flint."

I didn't have to be told, for I'd caught what Lew was thinking. In less than half a minute Flint Harrod moved away from his station opposite. He walked slower than Mel had, but he went to the corner and crossed toward the bank. Leaning a little farther out the window, I was in time to see the door to the bank swing open, and Flint step in.

"Let's go," Lew muttered, leaving the window to cross to the door to my waiting room.

He didn't answer when I asked him where we were headed, but led the way out to the platform at the top of the stairs. This platform was roofed over at the top, with its roof fitting flush against the rounded adobe wall of the bank.

Lew King reached up, caught hold, and swung himself up easily. In five seconds he was on the roof of the bank, reaching down to help me up.

"Mind tellin' me what the play is?" I asked, as soon as I crouched beside him up there.

"There's a skylight up here," he told me. "We're goin' to see what business Flint has with Mel Brand."

He was pulling off his boots as he spoke, so I sat down beside him and took mine off, too. Once I saw Lew pause to listen to shouts coming from up the street. After that he moved fast, whispering: "Hurry it up, Doc. There's not much time."

A skylight is one of those things that isn't noticed by one out of 100 people. But I remembered this one; many a time I'd seen Bill Crosson, in the center teller's cage in the bank, climb up on his counter on a hot day and reach up to pull a draw blind across the opening to cut out the glare of the beating sun.

Now we walked over to it, our feet moving soundlessly on the cool surface of the tarred flat roof. Lew lifted one hinged side of the skylight and it creaked a little as he eased it back. Then, looking down through the opening, my hopes were blasted when I saw the one-inch iron bars that ran across it. Naturally they were too narrowly spaced for a man to drop through them.

But Lew said — "Wait." — and hunkered down to look below.

Down there we could see dimly the outlines of the teller's cages, with the black square of the huge safe behind them, and, farther back, a patch of dimly lit flooring where the light came through from Mel Brand's office door.

Half a minute later I began to see the reason behind Lew King's telling me to wait. From down the street the shouts of the crowd grew louder, and suddenly there were shots, three of them blasting out above the din.

As though this was a signal, an angry roar echoed up from the crowd. They were storming the jail. There were more shots, and, as they blasted into the din, Lew King reached down, whispering to me: "Now's our chance, Doc."

Both of us took a hold on one of the bars below the skylight opening and pulled; I pulled until my muscles ached with the strain. Suddenly the bar gave way and came loose with a loud cracking as the wood frame in which it was imbedded tore loose. Lew lifted the bar out and laid it on the roof, and we both looked down again.

We heard Mel's office door open below, and even with the roar of the crowd the silence down there was real. We saw Mel's shadow move across the opening, and waited as he waited, unmoving.

Then we heard his voice. "It must have come from outside," he muttered. And with that the light was cut off again and we knew that he'd closed his door.

There was room now for us to climb down. Lew was first. He swung through and dropped onto the counter below without a sound. I was beside him ten seconds later. And together we eased open the door to Bill Crosson's teller's cage and silently walked on back until we stood to one side of Mel Brand's office door.

It was ajar, and, as we listened, I heard a strange voice say: "Then it'll be next Thursday night. We drive the herd out of the girl's upper pasture and into the brakes. Same place as it was before."

"One thing more," came Mel Brand's voice. "I don't care about feed this time. Those critters can die if they have to. It's up to you, but I want it played fast. Two days is the limit. By then you're to have your men out of the country."

Flint's low laugh echoed hollowly. "For two thousand I'll be out of the way in one day. This is easy money, Mel."

"You'd better be more careful than you were the other day," Mel said. "By bein' careless and leavin' your sign the other day, you did me a good turn. It was a piece of bull luck that Bud ran onto that sign. He was suspicious, anyway. His death is as pretty a frame on Lew King as I could have hoped for."

"Why are you doin' this other, Brand? You've got the mortgage on the outfit. You can foreclose."

"I could," Mel answered. "But I want what goes with the outfit. The girl."

Flint chuckled softly. "I see. You're afraid she wouldn't marry the man who kicked her off her own spread, eh? By liftin' her herd, she can lay the blame on somebody else instead of a skinflint banker. You're playin' a long chance, Brand."

"She'll come around," Mel purred.

"Well, in a week now you'll be sittin' pretty. This time King is framed so it'll stick. Four years ago, when you had me drop his runnin' iron alongside the trail out in the brakes, I wasn't so sure. You were lucky then."

"It wasn't luck. The iron was found, recognized, and damned near hung King. I planned it all out. I wanted that girl then, I want her now . . . an' I'm going to get her."

Then was when I moved, for those brief words had answered every question in my mind about Bud's death and about Lew's being framed.

I started to step into the doorway, but Lew stepped in beside me, kicking the door open and shoving me aside with one hand so that I lost my footing and sprawled to the floor out of his way.

The light flooded out of the room to frame his wide-shouldered figure, the .45 in his hand. A split second later his weapon roared in a stab of orange flame. And I was on my feet as he lunged into the room.

I had no part in that for seconds. Things happened too quickly. I saw Mel Brand rising out of his chair behind his desk with a gun in his blunt fist. It bucked as I watched, and then all hell cut loose.

Flint Harrod stood to one side of Mel's desk and Lew's pistol smashed down across his upswinging arm, and Flint's shriek cut in on the blast of his weapon as it spun from his hand. Then Lew was whirling on Mel Brand, meeting the thundering concussion of Mel's second shot.

I saw Lew jerk, saw him double up as the bullet slammed into him and his gun fell from his hand. But that hand streaked out to clamp on Mel's wrist. As Lew fell, he rolled into Mel, and the two of them piled onto the floor behind the desk.

An instant later, Flint Harrod stooped and snatched up his six-shooter from the floor. I swung up my own weapon then, thumbed back the hammer — and heard it *click* down on an empty chamber. The gun I had taken from Tom Nelson's office wasn't loaded!

Flint was taking aim as I whipped back my arm and threw my useless weapon, following it with my body as I lunged. The six-shooter caught him on the shoulder, and he flashed a startled glance back at me as I crashed into him.

He was like a bundle of steel springs. As he fell, he kicked back with his spurred heels and raked my shins. On the floor, my weight wasn't enough to keep him from wriggling away. But I got a hold on his crippled arm and twisted it, doubling it behind him until he suddenly stiffened, screaming with the torturing pain of it.

On the heel of that scream I struck Flint a full, hard blow in the face that made him go limp. At that instant a deafening blast ripped out from behind the desk. I rolled over so that I could look over there. Lew lay on top of Mel's huddled figure, neither of them moving. . . .

Later, Tom Nelson told me how the mob had broken into the jail and found him. And how they'd heard the shots from the bank just as they were unlacing the ropes I had tied around him.

He had run to the bank with the rest, and helped them break down the door. And he was the first to reach Mel's office — where he found me working over Lew King.

He sent someone up to my office after my black bag.

Before it came, Laura Pierce had pushed her way through the crowd and was standing at the office door, looking in at me with a crazy fear showing in her eyes. I couldn't blame her, for Lew King's face was as pasty-looking as a dead man's.

"Has he a chance?" she asked.

I nodded, not wanting to let on what I

was thinking then.

But Lew fooled me. Laura helped me get the bullet out — it was lodged under a shoulder blade — and he didn't develop the lung hemorrhage I'd expected.

Late the next afternoon, Lew opened his eyes. Laura was there with him, so I left.

Tom Nelson and I got very drunk that night.

DESERT DRIVE

When Jon Glidden was discharged from the U.S. Strategic and Tactical Air Force following the end of the Second World War, he returned to New Mexico and resumed his writing career. His serials would eventually be featured in *The Saturday Evening Post* where customarily authors were paid $50,000 for serial rights. He also continued to write short novels and short stories for the magazine market, primarily for Popular Publications' Western magazine group. "Desert Drive" was completed in January, 1947 and appeared in *Fifteen Western Tales* (6/47). The author was paid at the top rate the magazine offered and received $225.

I

He sat on the crest of the rocky slope, hot and winded from the long climb, and unbuttoned the collar of his flannel shirt, unsuspectingly laying bare his throat to the bullet that was to kill him. He was reaching out to lean the Winchester against the side of an outcrop when suddenly his fingers clawed rigidly open, letting the rifle fall. That was all he knew about it. The sound of the shot was swallowed by the wind howling up the cañon that was miles from anywhere. It was better than a quarter hour before the man who had killed him could cross from the cañon's far side and climb to where he lay. It took another hour and a half for the killer to carry him down through the rocks, rope him to his saddle, and lead his mare the three miles to a tunnel entrance, along a far deeper cañon. By that time a gusty rain had started lashing down out of the gray sky, the prospect of the storm's fierceness relieving the killer of the need for hiding sign.

Things were fairly simple after that. Back along the drift from the mine entrance, the killer took Giant Powder from a cache he knew was there. He put the body just inside the mouth of the drift and set his overly generous charge in a new and shallow offshoot nearby. The blast, heavy as it was, couldn't have been heard a quarter mile away in the rush of wind and rain.

That night the riderless mare drifted back to Singletree's corral, the crew left their bunks, and the hunt for Morgan Blake began. Along toward morning the killer himself joined the searchers over in Alder Cañon, where Morgan had yesterday told his daughter Laur he would be hunting deer. At mid-morning, with the rain settling to a steady drizzle, someone played a hunch and swung over to Morgan's mine to take a look.

So they found the tunnel caved in and they found Morgan after four hours of digging. He was badly mangled and the general feeling was summed up by his brother Tom, who said bitterly: "Damn' this place anyway! Morg should have stuck with the game he knew instead of playin' around with this fool thing. His luck just ran out."

You could have drawn a fifty-mile circle about Singletree on the day of the burying and you'd have found few people in that circle, except for youngsters and ailing old folk, who weren't there in the pines behind the house to see Morgan laid beside his wife in the grave. Even Fred Byrne came down from his lonely high country hide-out and was unmolested by the sheriff.

Laur stayed calm as she had been through the whole tragic affair, saying some nice things to the many who tried to tell her how her father's death had saddened them. She had a lot of the Blake iron in her, for the day after the funeral she was out with the crew from dawn to dark, seeing the sleek fat steers of Singletree's shipping herd well on their way to the low country and the trail around the desert.

That night, with Laur back home, shots blasted out of the night into the trail camp, and in the confusion the herd was stampeded and the chuck wagon set afire. Jeff Short, Singletree's ramrod, brought the news to Laur himself. She was at the breakfast fire before it was yet light, when Jeff split the crew — four men to try and pick up the sign of whomever had done the shooting, the other three to start rounding up the scattered whitefaces.

Laur rode at sunup with Jeff and the others, looking for sign. They found it within the hour. From what Jeff could tell, at least six riders had met below Squaw Ridge during the night and struck straight south for the desert. So they set out to follow that sign, and by ten, riding the parched country below the foothills, they sighted a man afoot lugging a saddle slung across his back.

They spotted this man from a good half mile away and Jeff planned carefully how they would come up on him, sending a pair of his men on a wide circle. Jeff rode straight on down with his carbine slanted across the saddle.

When he reined in twenty feet short of the stranger, he said: "Just drop that, mister. And lift your hands."

The look on the stranger's aquiline face had been pleasant and open. Now his expression tightened, became even leaner as he let go the saddle horn and slowly brought his hands up to the level of his wide shoulders. His eyes were gray and they lost their smiling look now for a veiled wariness — nothing else. Catching this, Jeff wondered if he was wrong in having judged him in his middle twenties. It took time to learn to wear a mask.

Jeff just sat there, saying nothing while the rest rode in on him. He didn't let his glance stray, either, having read a strong danger signal in the stranger's quiet manner, in the sure way he moved his rangy length and in the holster thonged low at his thigh. He idly noticed the alkali dust that powdered the man's outfit, the flush of a strong burn on skin already darkened by sun and wind, and a slight puffiness about the eyes and mouth that were signs of thirst. And he wondered if he had ever before seen a pair of shoulders as wide as this man's.

Bill Dooley and Laur were the first to join

him, and he told Dooley to get the stranger's gun. Only when the .44 Colt had been lifted from holster did Jeff let the Winchester's hammer down off cock and drawl: "Now, my friend, let's hear your story. Make it good."

Before the stranger could speak, Laur said: "Why waste time, Jeff? You know you hit one of their horses last night. This has to be the man. Just bring him on in."

"I'd like to hear him try and talk his way out of it," Jeff said, still looking at the stranger. "Go ahead, mister. How'd you get here?"

"Hoofed it from out there in the *malpais* on the desert."

"From exactly where?" Jeff asked.

The stranger turned and looked into the blue haze that veiled the detail of the waste country. "Across there's a peak standing all by itself. I came on a line with it and the big mesa above here."

"From where?"

"Alkali."

"Lose your jughead?"

The stranger nodded.

Jeff leaned lazily against the saddle horn, drawling: "You're a liar on two counts. First, you were with the bunch that hit our camp last night. I nicked your horse with some lead and you sided the rest as far as you could out into the desert before he dropped. Second, a man could almost never come across here from Alkali this late in the year. Cottonwood Seep's dry. There's no water."

The stranger's face relaxed in a grin that Jeff tried not to like. "So I found out," he said. "That's what they told me across there . . . almost never. I figured it was worth a try."

"If you're not lyin' . . . and you are . . . then you must've been in a hurry," Jeff said.

"Maybe I was."

Alongside Jeff, Laur cut in coolly: "You don't believe that, Jeff?"

"No." Jeff wasn't quite telling the truth, for he had his doubts. His glance settled on the stranger again and he asked: "You claim you made camp down below last night?"

The nod the stranger gave was quick enough, maybe a shade too quick.

"Hear anyone go by in the night?" Jeff wanted to know.

Again the stranger's head gave that brief tilt. "Along about three this mornin'. Six men, according to how I read the ground. They weren't wasting any time."

"Jeff," Laur said, "he's got it down too pat. Of course, he'd say he heard them if he was one of them and knew we'd sooner or later pick him up."

Jeff breathed a long sigh and nodded to Dooley. "Give him your jughead, Bill. You can climb up behind me."

Dooley led his roan in alongside the stranger and handed him the reins. As the stranger was tying his saddle on behind Dooley's, he looked across at Laur, asking: "Just what am I supposed to have done, miss?"

"You'll find out," was Laur's stubborn answer, as unsatisfactory to her as it was to the stranger. The way he kept on looking at her only heightened her anger. She had a lot on her mind, more than most women could have faced, and she was going at this blindly.

The stranger swung up onto Dooley's horse, finding the stirrups a good bit short. He eyed Jeff without lifting rein, saying: "You could prove my story by telegraphin' the hotel across at Alkali. My handle's Bob White. They can find it in their book."

"We got bobwhites in this country," Dooley now said in his dry way, adding significantly: "We also got whippoorwills."

Laur, encouraged by Dooley's remark, said: "Anyone could write your name in a hotel book. You'd all have some sort of story thought up before setting out on a thing

236

like this."

"Like what, miss?" Bob White asked.

"Like shooting up our herd last night," she told him, brown eyes blazing. Then, on nothing but a hunch, she said: "You ride for Fred Byrne, don't you?"

"Who's Fred Byrne?" The stranger's puzzlement appeared genuine.

"Give it up, Laur . . . give it up," Jeff said tiredly. He put his horse around behind the stranger's, drawling: "You go first, Bob White."

They headed for Tom Blake's layout because it was closest — and because, now that Morgan was gone, Laur would be looking to her uncle for help in a lot of ways, ways such as this.

Remembering what Jeff had called the girl, Bob White was thinking: *So Laur's not a man.* He knew the name; it was mentioned in a letter he now carried, and it tied in with his reason for having ridden five days to reach this country. For some minutes now he considered showing the letter, letting these people know who he was. But in the end he decided not to. Until he knew the reasons behind this odd circumstance of their having made him a prisoner, he wouldn't know who he could trust.

They were gradually climbing to higher

country, and after the first hour, deep in the foothills, they came to a trail and followed it. Presently, reaching a fork in that trail, Bill Dooley called out from behind: "Take the left one, Will!"

Bob looked around at him, drawling: "Will?"

"Sure. Short for whippoorwill," Dooley said.

His reply and its meaning put a broad smile on Bob's angular face. As he went on, he was still wondering what backed the meager details he had gathered from their conversation so far. The girl was pretty much in his thoughts, for she had shown him more animosity than the others. Obviously something important had happened to sharpen their tempers and they suspected him of being involved in whatever it was.

Just past noon they came to the hill fold where Bellows, Tom Blake's headquarters, sprawled by the creek. They found Blake at home, met him in the yard before the big H-shaped house. They had no sooner started talking with him than his foreman, Clyde Mould, sauntered over from the office and listened in.

Pretty soon, with a word here and there, Clyde was taking the thing out of Jeff's hands entirely, as was his way. He was a big, impulsive man with a head too large for his hat size, according to Jeff's way of thinking. He and Jeff just got on, nothing more, with no friendliness between them.

Bob took all the questions, Tom Blake's and Clyde's, calmly as ever a man could. But when Clyde started easing over toward him, asking — "Which way did Byrne drive those critters, stranger?" — the wariness Jeff had noticed so strongly again settled across his lean face.

He was answering Clyde's question — "The name Fred Byrne means nothin' . . ." — when Clyde swung on him.

The blow would have knocked a yearling flat. It caught Bob at the juncture of neck and shoulder and he was out before he hit the ground, slid a foot, and rolled onto his back.

Clyde said wonderingly: "Didn't mean to hit him that hard. Someone get a bucket of water."

He stood there, looking down at Bob curiously, like he was studying an odd hoof print or a poisonous weed he'd never seen before. He looked bigger than ever to Jeff, the two .45s slanted at his hips seeming small against his massive bulk.

"That's no way to go about it," Jeff said, and Laur backed him tartly.

"No, that gets us nowhere, Clyde." Her voice shook a little.

But Tom Blake drawled: "I'm not so sure." As their surprised glances came around to him, Blake went on: "This man's pretty sure of himself. None of us has ever laid eyes on him, which means he could be travelin' with Byrne's wild bunch." He gave Jeff a serious look as he said: "Maybe it's lucky for us you wounded his horse last night. So far he's the only thing we have to go on. Let Clyde work on him." He heard Laur catch her breath and told her: "I know you don't like the sound of it. I don't, either. But we don't have much of a choice. He won't talk without some persuasion."

They listened to him and reluctantly agreed, as was their habit in most things he advised. Tom Blake had more than white hair and an honest face to back his word. His Bellows-branded steers had been the first to graze this lush hill country. Years ago his straight thinking and cool-headedness had settled a range war before it got out of hand. People didn't forget things like that. Nor did they forget that he had served a term as sheriff and then a decade as judge of the district court with such fairness and brilliance that his decisions had become a part of the law of the country, more than the original statutes. So now they accepted Tom's suggestion without questioning it.

Presently Dooley came across from the well, lugging an oak bucket, and Clyde dumped its contents straight into Bob's upturned face. Bob took some of the water in his mouth and it was his gagging that brought him around. He lay there a long moment, staring straight up at the sky, his eyes slowly gaining comprehension. Then he pushed up onto an elbow, shook his head, and wiped the water from his face and sandy head.

He looked up at Clyde. A slow grin crossed his face but didn't change the wintry look in his eyes as he drawled: "A gold eagle says you can't do that again."

"Get on your feet and find out," Clyde told him.

So Bob picked himself up and stood, swaying like he was ready to go down again. Clyde stepped in on him again and swung hard, as hard as before.

Suddenly Bob twisted inside Clyde's reach, letting the bigger man's fist graze his shoulder. He straightened his left into Clyde's stomach, all his turning weight behind the blow. Then, when Clyde doubled over, groaning sharply, he lifted Clyde's head with a hard right, lifted it far back with such force that his watchers heard the sharp *crack* of his knuckles against Clyde's square jaw.

Clyde fell into him and he twisted away to let the Bellows ramrod go down sideways. Clyde lay there, writhing, spitting blood. Bob, not even breathing hard, looked at Tom Blake and drawled: "Do you reckon I can ever collect on that?"

Blake said solemnly: "You've made yourself a real enemy."

Laur, watching all this, seeing the stranger's sureness and the laughter now in his eyes, felt the same rise of anger as at her first sight of him. Now, without thinking, she reached across and pulled Bob White's .44 from Dooley's belt and lined it.

"You're going to take a beating for that," she breathed.

But she was wrong. Clyde was in no shape to give Bob a licking — they had to carry him to the bunkhouse — and no one else was inclined to substitute for him.

It wound up by Dooley and two Bellows hands riding off down the town trail with Bob. Shortly after they were out of sight, Tom Blake and two more of his men left to help the rest of Singletree's crew gather their scattered herd.

Jeff didn't go with them. Instead, he rode

back downcountry to the spot where they'd met Bob. Then, instead of following the sign of the riders who had shot up the herd, he put his horse along the line of the stranger's footprints, showing clearly in the sand.

He followed them with slow, methodical, trail-wise caution.

II

Dry Springs' sheriff was known best for having a quiet tongue. Homer Juling was thin as a rail, durable as a cedar fence post, and as good a sheriff as had ever served the county.

Dooley found him eating supper at Hattie Waggoner's rooming house, and he finished a second helping, ate his pie, and downed three cups of coffee before he came along the street to the jail where Dooley and the others waited with their prisoner.

Tilting the barrel of his Winchester at Bob, Dooley told Juling: "We came on this jasper hoofin' it near the sign left by the bunch that shot up the herd last night. Jeff's pretty sure he hit one of their jugheads during the ruckus, which is probably why our friend here was wearin' out his boots. Calls himself Bob White. You can make the warrant out in Tom Blake's name."

The sheriff commented with a grunt on

his way across the office to unlock the door of the single cell. Only then did he look at Bob and point to the cell with a lift of his narrow chin.

Bob walked in through the opening in the steel grating and stretched his flat length on the rickety cot, noticing the dust that lifted from the blanket and drifted out across a wedge of late sunlight slanting through the cell's west window. He was tired and hungry, but above all he was thirsty, dry inside and out after yesterday's and last night's parching that had cost him a fine gelding. But for a time he put that out of his mind, paying strict attention to what Dooley and the two Bellows riders were saying to Juling. For the first time, as the talk went on, he understood exactly what had happened and why they had been so suspicious of him.

Dooley and the other two finally left and rode away up the street. Juling came back alongside his desk and peered into the cell through the weakening light, asking finally: "Et yet?"

"No," Bob answered.

The sheriff went out and Bob lay back, thinking over today and yesterday, remembering how lucky he'd been. He had seldom felt worse than last night when, seeing the gelding couldn't make it, he had used a bullet as he hoped he never would again. Yes, he'd been in a hurry, as he'd halfway admitted this afternoon.

Just then Homer Juling's arrival with a pan of stew and a bucket of water cut in on his thoughts. The lawman motioned him away from the door and unlocked it long enough to set pan and bucket inside the cell. Bob emptied a dipper of water and was drinking the second even before the lawman had lit the lamp on his desk against the fading light.

When he had finished his meal, Bob rolled a smoke and said: "Maybe I'll stay on here. That was good grub."

Juling leaned around the corner of his battered roll-top and held out a hand. Bob reached the stew pan to him through the bars, noticing for the first time a round of firewood precariously propping up the desk's front corner where a leg was missing.

"How soon will they turn me loose?" Bob queried.

The sheriff thought a moment, shrugged.

"Who's the Fred Byrne they mention, Sheriff?"

"Outlaw," came Juling's meager reply.

Bob frowned, asking: "You let him run around loose?"

Juling's smile was a humorless rearrangement of his face's contours.

"This girl they call Laur. Who's she?"

Juling scowled for a time, then abruptly said: "Morgan Blake's daughter. They buried Morgan two days ago."

The words laid a visible shock through Bob. It took him several moments to frame his next question. "Then she's related to the Blake who owns that layout where they took me?"

Juling again let a nod do for words.

Bob looked down at the tip of his cigarette, purposely not glancing the sheriff's way as he drawled: "So this is the second jolt she's had lately. Her father murdered and now a beef herd run off."

"It was accident, no murder," Juling said quickly, giving this stranger some credit for being able to drag words out of him.

Bob looked up. "What kind of accident?"

"Blasting. Caved his prospect hole in on him."

"So?" Bob turned away, hiding the speculative look that came to his face.

The lawman came erect now, irritated and wanting to forestall any more talk. He turned the lamp low, took a final look at his prisoner, patted his coat pocket to be sure he had the cell key, and said briefly: "I'll bring Byrne in tomorrow."

He blew out the lamp and went out the door, not bothering to lock it, because he never did.

Bob pinched the glowing end from his smoke and in half a minute took out paper and tobacco and absent-mindedly rolled another. He was thinking: *So I was just two days late,* wishing now he had asked a few more questions to fill in the missing details of Morgan Blake's death.

As he flicked alight a match to put to the cigarette, he took the frayed letter from a slit pocket in his jeans and once more read it. He hadn't tried to hide it; his captors simply had missed it. But now it added nothing to the things he already knew.

He was holding the corner of the letter over the match flame when some sixth sense cautioned him against burning it. He folded it, and again returned it to his pocket. In the dying flare of the match, he looked down through the cell bars at the round of wood upended under the corner of the desk, noticing it now with a particular attention as the room went dark.

The wood was thicker than his forearm and he had seen that it was oak. Had it been a length of pine that would easily break, or cedar that would split, he would have immediately forgotten it. But now he went to his knees and reached through the bars trying to touch it. The faint last light of day coming from the street window was strong enough to let him see that his reach was a foot short. So he pulled the cowhide belt from the top of his waist overalls and tossed the buckle around the bottom of the round so that it swung back within his reach.

The quick pull he gave the belt jerked the round loose. The desk swayed a moment, toppled forward. The crash it made as it struck the floor rattled the cell's steel door.

Working fast, he pulled the round of wood through the bars and pushed it under the blankets of the bed. He had just buckled his belt and was standing there, taking a deep drag on his smoke, when boots pounded the plank walk outside and the door burst open.

A match flared alight at the front of the office and he saw Jeff Short standing there, looking across at him. There was the strong taint of coal oil in the air and Jeff surveyed the shambles of the overturned desk, the broken lamp, and the papers strewn every which way before he said mildly: "Thought I heard a bang in here. Juling's been goin' to have that thing fixed for months. Now maybe he'll do it."

He sauntered in across the office. The

match guttered out, and, as he struck another, he was standing almost within arm's reach of the cell door. He looked in at Bob squarely, drawling: "This afternoon I took me a ride. Out onto the desert. I found a horse carcass out there in a patch of mesquite. A sorrel jaw-branded Circle Dot. Nice animal."

"He was even better than he looked," Bob said.

Jeff was frowning as the second match burned out. That frown tied in with what he said, standing there in the dark. "Last night I was sure one of those jugheads stopped a hunk of my lead."

Bob waited for more. When it didn't come, he drawled: "My sorrel had a bullet through the head. Figure out how he could have carried me down to the desert from where your herd was last night and I'll own up to bein' this Fred Byrne's right-hand man."

"That's going to take some figurin'," Jeff admitted.

Bob was wishing there was light enough for him to catch Jeff's expression, but all he could make out was the man's vague shape against the fading rectangle of the street window. Adding Jeff's last words to what he had already decided about the man this afternoon, he said: "Your sheriff claims they buried Morgan Blake a couple days ago. Claims he had an accident with blasting powder. Does anyone think it mightn't have been an accident?"

"No one's said so," was Jeff's cautious answer. "Why?"

"Just wondering," Bob said.

"You're more than just wonderin'," Jeff countered, an edge to his voice. "What do you know about Morgan if you're a stranger here?"

"Did I say I knew anything?"

"The same as."

"You're loco, friend," Bob drawled. "Along with what happened to your beef herd last night, it's natural to wonder about the other. If a stranger would think to ask that question, you might have thought of it."

"Maybe I have," Jeff said, speaking more mildly now, in proof that the explanation satisfied him. "But Morgan didn't have enemies. Besides, he was so messed up from the explosion and all the rock that came down on him, there wasn't much left to look over."

"There wouldn't be."

"What d'you mean?"

"I mean there wouldn't be much left of him if someone planned a killing like that."

"Listen, brother," Jeff said softly, brittlely, "you may be in here without good cause. But don't go spreadin' talk like that around or they'll keep you here till you grow a long white beard. Morgan Blake was foolin' with something he didn't know enough about. He'd gone a little crazy with thinkin' he was going to run into gold. He laid too big a charge in that tunnel and didn't know enough to get clear when he set it off."

"Sure. You're probably right."

"By God, you better think I'm right! Suppose you spend the night practicin' not to let your tongue go loose. I rode in here to tell Juling to turn you loose. Now I've changed my mind."

Bob said nothing. Shortly he saw Jeff's shadow wheel around and head for the door. He let Jeff get almost to it before he said: "And am I supposed to think what happened last night was accident?"

Jeff halted and turned slowly around. "Who said it was?" When Bob made no reply, he repeated: "Who said it was an accident?"

"No one. But the two might tie in together."

"How?"

"I wouldn't know. It's not my affair. But if

251

it was, I'd be damned sure they didn't tie in."

"How could they?"

Bob thought a moment before drawling: "The girl runs that layout now. Who wants to get it away from her?"

"Not a soul."

"Think again."

"OK," Jeff said. He struck another match and held it high, looking back into the cell. "Three men have made Laur offers on Singletree. I'm one, her uncle's another, and Fred Byrne is the third. Now go on from there."

Bob gave a shake of the head. "You go ahead. I don't know enough about it."

"Tom Blake's a rich man," Jeff offered. "He'd pay more than the place is worth just to see Laur well fixed. I'd pay a fair price for the same reason."

"And Byrne?"

"The law's left him on the loose so long he's decided to turn respectable."

"What's he wanted for?"

"A killing in Texas. Rustlin' here."

"Juling says he's going up after him tomorrow."

"The hell you say," Jeff muttered.

Bob waited for more. Presently it came.

Jeff said: "Wonder what got Homer's

252

dander up?"

"Dooley telling him that Tom Blake thought Byrne did the shooting last night. Blake must cast a big shadow in this country."

"Plenty big," Jeff said. "And don't you. . . ."

His words broke off as a quick drum of hoofs sounded suddenly close by along the street. The hoof beats suddenly took on a thundering note, and, knowing that the horse out there was now running along the street's plank walk, Bob took sudden warning and wheeled away from the cell door, diving to the floor.

A shotgun's double charge blasted the front window out with a jangling roar. Buckshot struck sparks from the cell's door and back rock wall. The hollow pound of the fast-running horse broke to a muffled note as the animal hit the dirt of the street again and went swiftly away.

Bob edged over and looked through the bars, half expecting to see Jeff's sprawled shape remain on the floor. But in the faint light he saw him coming to his feet. Then the other was cursing with such blistering acidity that Bob knew he was all right.

Jeff's oaths broke off abruptly and he said: "Someone's goin' to a lot of trouble to see you're good and comfortable in here. I'd better get Homer to turn you loose so you won't go soft."

"Any ideas on who it could have been?" Bob asked.

"Not a one."

Bob heard men running along the walk now and said quickly: "Forget that about the sheriff turin' me loose."

"Why?" Jeff asked.

"I'd like to play it out the way it is now. If it's just the same to you."

Jeff had only time enough to say — "Suit yourself, White. But damned if I get it." — before a pair of men pushed the door open.

There was a lot of talk as others arrived, Homer Juling with them. Someone brought a lantern, and by its light the lawman surveyed the ruin of his office and his capsized desk, saying finally: "Hell with it." He turned to Bob. "You all in one piece?"

Bob nodded, noticing that Jeff was regarding him quizzically. Juling started waving the crowd out the door.

Presently, with a last look in at his prisoner, the lawman closed the door and Bob was listening to his plodding steps fade along the walk. In two more minutes the street was as quiet as it had been a quarter hour ago.

Bob pulled the length of oak from beneath his blanket and moved the cot over under the cell's small, high window. He stood on the bed and thrust the oak round between the window's two middle bars, then lifted a knee to push against the round's smooth sawed end. To give more leverage, he took a hold on the two outer bars as he pushed with his knee. He increased the pressure against the length of oak carefully, feeling the bars give slightly. Suddenly the rock-imbedded sill of thick wood split open with a loud *crack*.

Bob quickly pulled out the two center bars. He picked his hat off the bed and, with it protecting his hand, pushed out the pane of glass beyond the bars. He was belly down across the sill and worming his way out over the splintered sill almost as soon as the jangling sound of the glass falling into the back alley had died out.

He reached down, found his hands short of the ground. He let go with his knees, and dropped from the window on one shoulder, quickly rolling to a crouch. He stayed that way for several seconds, breathing shallowly, listening. Then, hearing no sound, he walked quickly up along the alley, keeping close to the rear of the buildings facing the street. He was well beyond the jail and heading for the squat shadow of a small barn, with a lean-to close to his left, when a voice spoke to him softly out of a passageway between two stores.

"Your jughead's tied there along that fence."

The instant that voice sounded, Bob made a dive toward the thick obscurity of the lean-to, going flat to the ground against the nearest wall. Now, although feeling a little foolish, he nevertheless lay still as he called: "Why all the help, Jeff?"

"Why not?" Jeff's low chuckle echoed across as he added: "That hunk of wood was missin', or Homer's desk wouldn't have gone down. You didn't want to be turned loose. So I reckoned you'd break out."

"How do you stand in this?"

"The same as you. I'm after some answers. Only you're goin' about it different from me. If anyone asks, no one helped you get that nag and your saddle out of Olson's corral."

"Thanks," Bob said. "One more thing. How do I get up to this Fred Byrne's place?"

"Follow the hill road north from town. There's a trail at the end of it. Byrne lives as far as that trail can take you. Only you won't ride right in on him."

"No?"

"No. Others have tried it. Clyde Mould was the last. Maybe you noticed the hole in his hat today. By the way, he's makin' talk about taking you apart. Better stay clear of him. He's mean."

"So Byrne doesn't take to Mould?"

"As well as he takes to anyone." Jeff was silent a long moment, then added: "But don't let that stop you. If you run onto anything, let me know."

"Where do I find you?"

"Our layout's three miles east of Tom Blake's."

Bob said — "OK." — and lay there waiting.

"Well, get started!" Jeff called shortly.

"After you," Bob told him.

Once more Jeff's soft laugh sounded across the stillness. "You're sure a trustin' soul," Bob heard him say before his steps slurred toward the street along the passageway, gradually fading out altogether.

When he was sure that Jeff had gone, Bob stood up and went on up the alley until he came to a fence. Back along it he found a Singletree branded bay horse tied to a post. His own saddle was loosely cinched to the animal's back. Looped around the horn were his shell belt and horn-handled .44.

III

Twice during the next four hours Bob lost his way along false trails and wasted time riding back to find the main one. It was long past midnight when he swung up an off-shoot of a broad cañon he had been following and, for better than a mile, crossed and re-crossed a stream, pushing the bay through alder and willow thickets flanking it. A sprinkling of aspen was grayly lining the black backdrop of the pines when the offshoot broadened to show a high meadow, climbing gradually to the level of the flanking rims, its outline very faint in the starlight.

He was close in to the foot of the meadow when a sound rustled from a thick stand of cedar closely beside the trail. The bay's head came up and it whickered. Then a voice hailed — "Hold it!" — and Bob reined in, sitting very still in the saddle.

"Get rid of the iron," the voice directed with a flat-toned meaning.

Bob lifted out his Colt and tossed it into the grass closely alongside.

Shortly a man's indistinct shape materialized out of the blackness of the trees, asking: "Where you headed, neighbor?"

"To Byrne's place."

The man gave a muted, dry laugh. "Now

who would you be?"

"I'll tell that to Byrne," Bob drawled.

"Will you, now?" There was faint surprise in the man's voice. "Well, in that case, we better be goin'. Hold on a minute."

He walked over and picked up Bob's gun. Then his shadow faded back into the obscurity and shortly he reappeared, astride a rangy calico horse. He pointed on up the trail and Bob lifted rein, and they rode for some minutes until the trees fell away and there was grass to either side of them.

Halfway up the meadow, the guard commented tartly: "Fred's not goin' to like bein' routed out at this hour."

"He'll like it," Bob said.

"Now will he?" Again came the man's dry chuckle.

Above the meadow the trail cut through a thin stand of stately yellow-bark pine, crested a rise, and dropped steeply to cross the creek and climb again through a narrow slot close below the rim. Then, finally on a level with the rim, it swung hard left through spruce with bough ends shining silvery in the starlight. Bob caught the pungent taint of cedar smoke in the air and several moments later they came suddenly on a cabin.

It squatted darkly near the edge of the rim, the trees hiding it and running on back, so that it was hard to pick out a pole corral and a sideless barn close by.

"Get down and stretch," the guard drawled as he swung aground. He added — "Stay set." — and went in through the nearest of the cabin's two doors, leaving it half open behind him.

His voice and another, deeper-toned, sounded in there, and shortly the flare of a match outlined the door opening. A moment later the light strengthened as a lamp was lit and a man's shadow filled the doorway and remained there. Bob knew he was being watched.

Half a minute later the door swung wide and the guard called: "Come on in!"

Bob stepped into a small room, poorly lit by a shelf lamp with a smoked chimney. Under the single window at the back was a bunk, covered with rumpled blankets. At its foot stood a cartridge case littered with shaving essentials, a mail order catalogue, a cracked shard of mirror. Beyond, in the corner, a pot-bellied stove gave out only a hint of warmth.

The man who stood by the stove pushing shirt tails inside the belt of his waist overalls was stocky, black-haired, and dark-eyed. Around his waist hung a cedar-handled .38, a Smith & Wesson.

He gave Bob a long, enigmatic look, and then said tonelessly: "Well?"

Bob asked: "You're Fred Byrne?" Getting only a brief nod in reply, he went on: "First . . . you ought to know that Homer Juling's on his way up here after you this morning."

Byrne's look didn't alter in the slightest as he drawled: "Let him come. He's tried it before."

"Want me to hang around, boss?" the guard asked.

Byrne's head tilted in a brief nod. His eyes hadn't shifted from Bob. "Is that all?"

"No," Bob told him. "Last night somebody shot up a beef herd of Singletree's. Juling thinks you did it."

A flicker of interest, instantly gone, touched Byrne's eyes. His glance still holding to Bob, he said: "Harry, get down there on the trail. Take Braden with you."

The guard came across to the bed to toss Bob's .44 on the blankets, then went out. Bob heard the cabin's far door open, caught the muted sound of voices, and the soft closing of the door. Steps passed along the front of the cabin and faded into the stillness.

All this time Byrne had been watching him. Now the outlaw flatly queried: "That all you got on your mind?"

Bob said: "I came after help."

"What kind of help?"

"Did you shoot up that herd?" Bob asked.

"No."

Byrne's manner showed not the slightest interest in whether or not his reply was believed. Yet Bob did, strangely enough, decide that the man was telling the truth. So he said: "All right, you didn't do it. I'm trying to find out who did. It's more than a one-man job."

It was a long moment before the outlaw queried: "What stakes you got in this?"

"Today they picked me up down near the desert and tossed me in their *jusgado*, claimin' I was one of the bunch that threw the lead. Tonight I busted out of there. They'd talked about you, so I headed up here."

"For a hide-out?"

Bob nodded. "Partly. And partly because I thought you'd help run this thing down."

"Why the hell should I?" came Byrne's tart query.

"To clear yourself."

Now, for the first time, Fred Byrne's expression thawed a little from its cold set. Then, abruptly, he was smiling. His face looked much younger as he said: "Friend, they've saddled me with more dirty shenanigans than ten men could do in a lifetime. One more won't bust my back."

"It would, if they decided you killed Morgan Blake," Bob drawled.

Byrne's face froze in surprise. His hand fell to holster and there was a light of sudden fury in his eyes as he said: "Talk! And don't leave nothin' out. Morg Blake was the one friend I ever had down below. Who said he was murdered?"

"No one said it. It's just my hunch."

Bob took a chance then, hoping he had judged this man correctly. He drew the letter from his hip pocket and handed it across. The outlaw, after a puzzled look at him, took the page from the envelope, and read it. And as his eyes scanned the lines, some of the hardness left his face.

Finally he looked across at Bob: "You're this Angus White?"

"No. Angus was my father. He died a month ago. Morgan Blake couldn't have heard about it. He and the old man were partners years ago, before either of them married. When this trouble came along, he called on someone he knew he could trust."

"Which still doesn't tell me why you're here," Byrne said.

"Because it's what the old man would

have wanted me to do."

An odd expression crossed the outlaw's face as he returned the letter. For a long moment he stared at Bob vacantly, seeming hardly aware of him. Then, abruptly, he said: "You don't know it, but you've come to the right man, White."

Bob waited for more. And presently it came.

Byrne took a sack of tobacco from his pocket, built a smoke, and handed the sack to Bob, saying: "Like I said, Morg was my friend. In case you're askin' why, it's because he kept those jaspers down below off my neck. Last spring, he was up here one night when some beef was rustled down below. When they tried to hang the job on me, he must've told the sheriff that he had proof I hadn't done it. Juling must have listened, because next day, when he brought a posse up here, he came slow enough so I had plenty of time to get the crew out." The outlaw took a long pull at his smoke, eyeing Bob obliquely. Then he said: "Now about your idea on Morg bein' murdered. Where'd you get it?"

"The letter says someone had taken a shot at him before," Bob said. "Then that trouble they had with the herd last night looks queer. Add that onto Morgan being dead and it looks like someone's after the layout."

"Anyone else think the way you do? Juling, for instance?"

"I wouldn't know what Juling thinks. Jeff Short might, though."

Byrne's look was interested now as he asked: "You know Jeff?"

Bob nodded. "He was the only one that took the trouble to check my story. Tonight he helped me bust out of the jail after someone had tried to blow me apart with a Greener from the street."

The outlaw's brows lifted. "Did they?" he drawled, smiling wryly. "Now I reckon they'll be tryin' to tie a bushwhack onto me."

Bob said nothing, and Byrne turned and opened the stove door, throwing on several chunks of wood and then poking the coals to life. His back to Bob, he said: "I tried to make it up to Morg for what he'd done for me. This summer I heard he was foolin' with a prospect hole up Scalplock Cañon. So one day I drifted down there and paid him a visit. In an hour I'd told him more about hard-rock minin' than he'd learned in over a year." He glanced back at Bob, explaining: "My old man was a mine boss. So I did what I could for Morg. Which brings us to somethin' that may tie in with what you say about murder." He straightened, wiping the soot from his hands along his thighs. "About a week ago, Morg was up here, askin' me about a blastin' chore. He was workin' a new drift and he wanted to go deeper. I told him how to drill, to set his charges. One thing he said has stuck in my mind. 'I've got the place mucked out neat as a pin,' he says. 'Think I'll take off a day or two and hunt, breathe some fresh air for a change.' Two days later he was dead. And, sure enough, he'd gone huntin' like he said he would. It looks now like he got anxious to get back to work. You probably know he was found back there in his tunnel."

"You must've given him some poor advice," Bob said. "Otherwise, he wouldn't have died the way he did."

Byrne shook his head, a worried look crossing his blocky face. "It's damn' queer," he muttered. "I'd taught him plenty about Giant Powder. And he was careful. I've more than once thought like you, that maybe he cashed in different from what we think. But I couldn't go down there and tell 'em that."

"Why not?"

Byrne smiled crookedly. "Suppose it was murder and they found out I'd been helpin' Morg? Couldn't they claim I'd killed him because I knew he'd run onto something in his mine? Before any of this come to me, I'd made the girl an offer on Morg's layout."

"Had he run onto something?" Bob asked.

"A little. Not much, but enough to keep his hopes up."

"You wanted to buy Singletree? Why?"

"Because of the girl. Because I felt I owed Morg something for stickin' by me when it counted. And maybe because I'm sick of livin' up here, tryin' to make a livin' with the winters killin' off my profits and those outfits down below thinkin' I swing a sticky loop every time a bunch of steers wanders off. You can believe this or not, stranger," he added grimly, "but every dollar I got was made honest."

"How could you live at Singletree even if the girl would sell to you?"

"They don't want me down in Texas any more," Byrne said. "And with what I hope Morg told Homer Juling, I'd be willin' to take the chance the law down there would let me alone."

Into the brief silence came faint hoof strikes, suddenly echoing up from the cañon below. Bob saw Byrne stiffen, cocking his head to listen. Then the outlaw said urgently: "Harry couldn't be in that much of a hurry with Juling." He stepped to the bed, took Bob's .44 from the blankets, and held it out as he leaned over to blow out the lamp, saying quickly: "Get out there an' out o' sight. It could be I'll need you."

Nothing Byrne could have said or done would have convinced Bob more completely of the outlaw's trust in him. As he took the weapon and went to the door, the room suddenly going black about him, he knew Byrne had made the decision he had hoped for. *That makes three of us, Byrne, Jeff, and me* was his thought as he heard the sound of the running horses suddenly strengthen. Then, from the direction of the trail head, he caught the indistinct shapes of two riders running in on the cabin.

He had laid his palm against the handle of the Colt when suddenly the wariness drained out of him. For it was Harry, Byrne's guard, who called out: "Comin' in, Fred! Jeff Short's here to see you."

The door swung open and Byrne stood there, wiping alight a match along his thigh. Bob walked over to them as Jeff and Harry swung around, Jeff asking abruptly: "Where's Bob White?"

"Here," Bob answered.

Jeff swung around, saw Bob approaching, and asked in a harsh rush of words: "Why didn't I have sense enough to take you with me tonight? I'd no sooner got back to our camp than all hell started poppin'. They really did a job this time!"

"Who?" Bob asked. "What happened?"

"The Lord only knows who," Jeff answered ruefully. "But they burned twice the powder they did last night. Today's gather is scattered from hell to breakfast again."

Byrne, from the doorway, drawled: "Tell him I've been up here the whole time, White. Every man of the crew is here."

"That's right, Jeff," Bob said.

He heard Jeff's prolonged, helpless sigh. Then the Singletree ramrod was saying: "Maybe this thing's gettin' the best of me."

"Don't let it," Bob told him, adding: "Byrne's with us."

"How do you mean?" Jeff's glance swung to the outlaw's obscure shape there in the dark doorway.

"We'd better go in and talk over a few things," Bob said.

Shortly the lamp was once again thinning the shadows in the cabin's small room. And now Bob did most of the talking. He showed Jeff the letter, and, as Jeff read it, he gave Bob a smiling, surprised glance, saying: "Hell, I've heard of Angus White for years. So's Laur. All you'd had to do was show this when we picked you up and things would have turned out different."

"Maybe it's a good thing they didn't," Bob said.

Jeff frowned. "How do you figure that?"

"Right now only the three of us suspect what happened to Morgan Blake. Besides the killer, if there was one. If it got around who I was, this ranny would know I had a good reason for being here. As it is now, I'm just a nuisance, strayin' around, with maybe the law on my tail. No one'll pay much attention to me. Which gives us a chance to look around on the quiet with no one bein' any the wiser."

"Where we going to look?" Jeff asked.

Bob looked at Fred Byrne, asking: "Have you looked over Morgan's mine since he died?"

The outlaw shook his head.

"Then we start there," Bob said.

Jeff thought it over a moment, then gave a slow shake of the head. "We won't find anything we don't know already."

"Maybe we won't," Bob said. "But it's worth a try."

Jeff gave him an oddly respectful glance, drawling: "You've been travelin' under a plenty big head of steam ever since I laid eyes on you, White. How about slowin' down and gettin' some rest?"

"I'll sleep on the way down, if you can keep that horse you loaned me from wanderin'," Bob said.

In another quarter hour, he was doing exactly that as he, Jeff, and Byrne took the trail down off the rim.

Once, crossing the meadow, Jeff reined over close to Fred Byrne and said in a low voice: "Worse things could happen than havin' him along, Fred."

"I was thinkin' the same," was the outlaw's answer.

IV

When Laur saw Tom Blake riding in along the road that flanked the pasture that morning, an almost overwhelming feeling of gratitude gripped her. She had been up since midnight, had made the crew a big breakfast. Being alone with her thoughts the past three hours had for the first time in these trouble-packed days made her uncertain and afraid, really afraid.

The sight of her uncle, the way he sat the saddle, so erectly and solidly, reminded her of all the things he had done for her and of how she could count on him to help her now. Her relief was so keen, so sudden, that for a moment her feelings got the better of her and tears came to her eyes.

But she had her emotions well in hand when she walked out across the yard and met him at the tie rail. Holding the big red stallion's bit while her uncle swung aground, she said: "Tom, I was never so glad to see anyone. This thing's nearly got me."

"It's nearly got me," he said soberly.

"What have they found out? And where's Jeff?" she asked.

"They've found exactly what they did yesterday. The bunch that did the shooting last night headed straight for the desert. Lord knows where Jeff is. He lit out right after it happened without telling anyone where he was going. Clyde's managing things. This time they'll have an easier gather. Most of the critters ran up a box."

She took his arm as they turned up across the yard to the small L-shaped cabin, saying: "You're about ready for a second breakfast? We had buckwheat cakes this morning."

"I could eat a stack a foot high." His habitual reserve broke as he smiled down at her. Then, abruptly, his smile faded and he said solemnly: "You can't keep on like this, Laur. Why not let me take the whole thing off your hands?"

Until today the thought of anyone else owning Singletree had irritated Laur to a point of real anger. But this morning she had come to the realization that a woman had no place trying to fight the kind of trouble she was fighting. Neither she nor Jeff had even made a beginning of understanding exactly what they faced and it seemed now that it would take a big tough crew headed by a man like Clyde Mould to accomplish anything against the odds facing Singletree.

So now she said with a keen relief: "I'll have to give in, Tom. Singletree's yours any time you want it."

"Want it?" he echoed dryly. "You can't exactly say that I want it, Laur."

"I know. You're just being kind."

"Nor am I being kind, either," he said in his dignified way. "It's purely business, sound business. I'll get a good return on my investment, which is all a man can ask."

"Thirty thousand is too much, Tom. I'd be glad to get twenty-five."

"Women and business!" he snorted in mock exasperation, adding: "You let me decide what it's worth. You don't think I'd rob myself to do you a favor, do you?"

"That's exactly what you would do," she said. There was something about all this that continued to puzzle her and now she said: "You surely must have some idea of what

273

all this means. I don't."

He frowned thoughtfully and, in his careful way of reserving judgment, said: "There are several possibilities. Only one makes much sense."

"What's that?"

"Fred Byrne made you an offer, didn't he?" He waited for Laur's nod before continuing. "You wouldn't sell and he evidently wants the outfit badly enough to make you sell. The simplest way to do that is for him to make sure you can't ship any beef. You're in no position to carry these cattle through the winter. So all he has to do is keep your shipping herd off the trail that takes you around the desert to the railroad at Alkali. So far he's done it. You've doubtless noticed that he hasn't hurt anyone, hasn't shot up your men, or even your cattle."

Laur nodded soberly. "I've noticed that."

Tom Blake lifted his spare shoulders in a shrug. "So there you have it. Byrne seems the logical one to be behind this. I'm sure of nothing, understand. But, regardless, from now on you'll let me do the worrying. I want you to plan a trip back East at once. By the time you're back here, everything will be settled."

She pressed his arm tightly, saying:

"You're good to me. It's almost like . . . like you're taking Dad's place."

Back in the kitchen once more, Laur felt so much better that the room seemed a far brighter and more colorful place. She had started her uncle on his meal with a steaming hot cup of coffee and was ladling the buckwheat mix onto the range's griddle when she heard a horse trotting in toward the house.

Looking out the window, she saw who it was and said: "Jeff."

Tom Blake looked across at her with a scowl. "Which reminds me, Laur," he said. "About Jeff. I . . . I'd rather he didn't go with the outfit when I take over." He caught the hurt look that came to her eyes and quickly added: "Now don't get me wrong, honey. Jeff's a good man, one of the best. But he and Clyde don't get on too well and I can't let Clyde go in favor of him. Now, I've got that feeder layout down in Cimarrón and the man that bosses it never has made it pay the way it should. I want to put Jeff in charge. He'll draw better wages than he does here."

"But Jeff belongs here, Tom. He. . . ." She broke off as Jeff's step sounded on the back porch.

He came in hat in hand, a serious look on

his face. Without ceremony, he said: "We've run onto something you both better know about. It wasn't the blast there at the mine that killed Morgan, Laur."

She was too astonished to speak, but Tom Blake asked sharply: "What are you saying, man?"

Jeff nodded. "I'm right, Tom. We've just been up there. We moved away some of the rock near where we found Morg. We found a boot track. Morgan wore a small boot. These were bigger than his. Just average size."

"Who's we?" came Tom Blake's careful question.

"That stranger we picked up yesterday, Bob White. And Fred Byrne. It was White who thought of movin' the rock. . . ."

"Fred Byrne!" Tom Blake exploded.

Jeff nodded soberly. "This Bob White went up there to see Byrne, last night after he busted jail. The story he got from Byrne will take some believin'. But it seems. . . ."

Then he told them the story.

Bob and Fred Byrne were deep in the tunnel, looking over Morgan Blake's cache of Giant Powder in the glow of a screened coal-oil lamp.

"Eight cases," Byrne mused, frowning.

"That's a hell of a lot more than he ever kept up here before. Looks like he planned on doing a lot of shooting along that new drift."

"Let's have a look at the new one," Bob said.

They turned back along the tunnel.

The mouth of the new drift Morgan Blake had been working was half blocked by rubble brought down by the explosion. They climbed over it and walked the twenty feet to the end of the drift. Here, again, was a slanting heap of granite shards.

"He hadn't mucked out after settin' off his last charge," Byrne said idly, turning away.

"Which is sort of queer," Bob drawled.

The outlaw eyed him quizzically. "How come?"

"Remember what you told me last night?" Bob queried. "Morgan had been up to see you and said he had this place cleaned out and was ready for another blasting job. But he was going hunting before he started it. We know that he went hunting, that he died that day. So he couldn't have drilled and blasted."

Sudden understanding changed the look on Fred Byrne's face and he whistled softly. He stepped over and looked at several thin black lines that streaked the gray monotone of the granite's coloring.

"That's color," he said at once. "Not much. But it's what Morg was hoping would lead him to a vein of real pay dirt."

Bob nodded toward the rubble at the head of the drift. "You don't see those black streaks in what's lying there."

The outlaw went to his knees, picked up several shards of granite, and tossed them aside. He inspected several more, saying finally: "This isn't even from this part of the tunnel. Somebody wheeled this stuff here." He gave Bob an odd sidelong glance, asking: "Did you ever work hard rock, White?"

"No."

"Then you've got a damned sharp pair of eyes. Now what do we do?"

"Dig in behind this stuff and see what our friend was trying to hide, besides a murder," Bob told him.

They went back to the main drift for a shovel and it was Fred Byrne who, some ten minutes later, scooped aside the rubble halfway down along the head of the drift and let out a whoop that rang hollowly back along the tunnel.

He said excitedly: "Black as the inside of a boot and a good foot wide! More gold than I've ever seen in one vein!"

Bob was strangely unexcited. His hunch had paid off handsomely, yet he was oddly dissatisfied. Trying to put his feeling into words, he said: "We still don't know who did it."

The outlaw gave a slow shake of his head, and Bob went on: "Jeff's given me three men to pick from, the only three that made offers on Singletree. You, Jeff himself, and Tom Blake."

Byrne smiled crookedly. "You might as well join the rest in tryin' to hang me for it."

But Bob seemed only to have half heard and said: "You'd have been a fool to tell me what you did last night if you were the one. So you weren't. It could have been Jeff. If it was, I'm no judge of a man."

Byrne waited and, when Bob didn't go on, said: "Then that leaves Tom Blake. If you say he did it, I'll be the first to call you a liar."

"Then start callin'," Bob drawled. "Remember, Jeff was there in the jail when that shot came last night. If he hadn't hit the floor, it could have cut him in two."

"But Tom Blake's better off than any man this side of the desert. What would he want with more of anything?"

Bob shrugged. "Don't ask me how a

man's mind works when he can't be satisfied with more than enough."

"Then you're sayin' it is Tom Blake?"

"Not for sure yet," Bob said. He still hadn't pinned down his dissatisfaction.

He turned then and led the way out of the drift. Out in the clear, sun-bright air once more, they went straight down to their horses. Bob was reaching for the bay's trailing reins when the air whip of a bullet cut past his face.

He threw himself around and sideways as the flat *crack* of a carbine floated to them. As he moved, his right hand instinctively dropped and swept up along his thigh, palming out the Colt. Byrne, watching him, barely saw the gesture, as White threw two shots so closely spaced that they blended in one prolonged blast of sound. The branches of a thicket swayed and for an instant he glimpsed a man's hunched-over shape dodging beyond the thicket into the pines. He lined the .44 again but was too late. He wheeled, vaulted to the saddle, and raked the bay to a lunging run as Byrne ran for his horse.

The bay had taken only a dozen strides when a second shot cracked out of the pines. The bay's forelegs buckled and he somersaulted, throwing Bob clear. Bob hit the ground on his left shoulder and slid along the gravel, tearing the sleeves of jumper and shirt. His arm stung as he rolled to his feet, waving Fred Byrne on.

The rifle spoke sharply a third time. He turned in time to see Fred Byrne sway in the saddle. Byrne's buckskin gelding broke out of its run to a trot and slowly the other doubled over and swayed to one side. The gelding came to a stand as Byrne, breaking his fall with a grip on the horn, toppled from the saddle.

Bob caught the staccato pound of a fast horse going away downcañon as he was running across to Byrne. The buckskin had trotted on a few yards and stood now with trailing reins.

Fred Byrne's face was twisted with pain. He managed a wry grin. "What a . . . way to cash in! No fight. . . ."

"You'll be all right," Bob said quietly, trying to hide the conviction that Byrne was dying, for a red stain showed at the center of the outlaw's shirt front.

He heard sounds echoing up the cañon now that told him more than one horse was coming toward him. His hand dropped to his thigh, hung above the handle of the Colt an instant, came away again, for a pair of riders had come into sight beyond the creek.

Jeff Short was in the lead and several moments later Bob recognized Laur as the other.

They saw him kneeling there, and Jeff lifted his horse to a run, splashing across the creek with Laur close behind. They reined in a few feet away.

Bob glanced bleakly up at them, giving a meager shake of the head, asking Jeff: "Did you get a look at him?"

"Yeah." Jeff nodded and soberly said, "It was Clyde Mould."

V

They buried Fred Byrne there in the pines below the mouth of the tunnel where a windfall's roots had left a hole in the black earth. When they had finished, Jeff said simply: "He was a better man than any of us knew. He wouldn't like any fancy words said over him."

"If Dad could only have told us about him," Laur said gravely. "It seems unfair. . . ."

"He had a lot of enemies . . . and he was bitter," Bob told her. "But a good man will go a long way to help his friends. He figured he owed your father quite a lot."

"There's so much I don't understand, that I didn't know about," she said. "Now Jeff tells me you're Angus White's son. That Dad had written Angus about this."

Bob nodded and gave her the letter. And while she was reading it, he was closely studying her, quite suddenly realizing that he had been wanting to sharpen the image his mind's eye had carried of her since their meeting yesterday. He had thought of her countless times since then and this morning, trying to remember how she had looked, he had been annoyed that he couldn't with any exactness.

She seemed different today, more humble and more feminine than yesterday when anger had been so strong in her, and, if he had had any misgivings about wanting to be involved in this trouble that wasn't his, he forgot them.

At length Laur's eyes lifted to meet his and she said humbly: "Things would have gone so differently if I had only known. I'm sorry for the way you were treated."

A broad smile touched Bob's lean face and he drawled: "All I had to do was show you the letter. But it seemed better this way. I didn't know what I was in for . . . turned out you didn't, either. Have you seen your uncle?"

For a moment that angry look he knew so well flickered in her eyes. But then it died and a worried expression took its place. "Yes. I agreed to sell. I still don't think he's behind all this."

"Good," Bob said. "Only . . . don't sign anything for a few days."

"What'll that get us?" Jeff asked.

"Time to get the herd across the desert."

"Around, you mean," Jeff amended.

"No, I mean across," Bob stated. "How deep would a man have to go to strike water at that dried-up seep?"

Jeff frowned, thinking a long moment before he said: "Macklin was out there ten years ago in the winter and dug a well with the idea of puttin' in a stage stop. He found water at twelve feet. Then he went broke and nothin' more has ever been done about it. His well's caved in."

A look of relief eased Bob's expression and he asked: "How bad was the herd scattered last night?"

"Most of the stuff ran up a box. Right now the boys must have the herd pretty well in hand."

"Then you could move the herd out to-night?"

"If it would do us any good," Jeff said.

"It will," Bob told him. "Only you'll move it east, not west toward the low country. Be sure and tell Tom Blake and Mould that you're moving back onto your own range, if they get curious. Does Mould know that you saw him just now?"

Jeff shook his head. "He was lookin' over his back trail and we saw him just for a second. Why are we pushin' those critters back inside our fence?" he asked impatiently.

"So they can go straight through and down onto the desert tonight. Some time tomorrow morning they'll come in on that seep. And they'll have water."

Jeff's look was incredulous. "Where they going to get it?"

Bob tilted his head toward the tunnel opening above them, drawling: "There's enough Giant Powder up there to blow a hole clean through to China. Your steers can drink till the water runs out their ears, Jeff."

Tom Blake was at lunch when Laur and Jeff rode into the yard. Before they had tied their horses, he called to the cook to set two more places.

"Anything new?" he asked as he met them on the wide porch.

Jeff told of Fred Byrne's being killed.

Blake said solemnly: "I've evidently misjudged the man. You both believe his story of having helped Morgan work the mine?"

"Why shouldn't we?" Laur asked.

"I was only trying to get it straight in my mind . . . so I've been wrong all along about Byrne. It leaves us to make some other guess on who's behind all this."

Jeff gave him an enigmatic look of mild curiosity. Shifting his glance quickly to Laur, Blake saw that she was staring at him in wide-eyed expectancy, not even pretending to be interested in her food. Her face colored as he looked at her.

She asked: "What's Clyde been doing lately, Tom?"

Blake shook his head. "Funny you should ask that. Last night I wanted to see him along about time to turn in. He wasn't at the bunkhouse, and neither were four of the men. I couldn't sleep and was awake about midnight when they rode in. When I asked Clyde about it this morning, he said they'd been in a session of poker in town."

"Anything wrong with that?" Jeff asked.

Blake frowned. "No, perhaps not. But they usually stick pretty close during the week. Then this morning Clyde's been away somewhere when I thought he'd be with the baling crew in the meadow. Maybe he's playing detective on his own . . . if so, he may turn up something." He looked at Laur. "You must understand how anxious I am to help. You're my own flesh and blood, Laur. There's nothing I wouldn't do for you."

Laur looked quickly at Jeff, who shook his head.

Jeff said tiredly, resignedly: "Anything you turn up, let us know. Somebody saw Clyde this morning, near where Byrne was killed. Maybe, as you say, he was playing detective. I wanted to talk to him, but Laur an' I better be ridin'."

Blake walked to the tie rail and, as they left, told them: "If I learn anything about Clyde, I'll let you know at once."

Jeff and Laur were nearing the trees where the trail lifted out of the valley above the ranch before either of them spoke. And it was Laur who said abruptly: "You see, Jeff. He doesn't know about Clyde." Jeff looked obliquely across at her, nothing more, and she flared: "You don't think I'm right?"

"I didn't say that," he countered. He looked off through the trees, then turned in the saddle and glanced back along the trail. The valley was hidden now, and with a tilt of his head toward the timber above he asked: "Want to try something?"

"What?"

"Sit up here and look at what goes on below for a while."

Laur was puzzled. "Why, Jeff?"

"I can't help thinkin' how sure Bob was of his hunch on Tom. Little as I know Bob, it looks so far like it might pay for us to listen to him."

"He can be wrong, Jeff."

"Can be. But he hasn't been so far."

Laur thought about that a moment before she asked: "What do you want me to do?"

"Like I said, wait up here and keep an eye open. We might see something."

So they reined off the trail, and presently, their horses tied back in the timber, they were at the tree margin, looking down.

Jeff had barely had the time to roll and light a smoke before Laur exclaimed softly. Looking down there, he saw Tom Blake riding north from the corral, just disappearing into a thin stand of timber that separated Bellows' broad meadow from the barn lot.

"He's in a hurry," Laur said.

Silently they watched Tom Blake reappear on the far side of the trees and swing west. His horse was running and presently it was obvious that he was headed for the meadow's western end, where they could see four men working a hay baler inside a fenced half acre where the summer's crop stood in eight ranked haystacks.

Blake pulled his horse in and stopped

along the fence close to the baler. A man they hadn't seen before, a man looking far bigger than the others even at this distance, came from behind one of the stacks and walked over to Blake.

"It's Clyde," Laur breathed, and, glancing at her, Jeff saw the color drain from her face as she added unbelievingly: "After what he said about not knowing where to find Clyde."

In another minute they saw the Bellows ramrod turn and run across to several horses tied in the shadow of one of the stacks. He swung quickly astride a brown, rode out the fence gate, and joined Blake. The two of them headed back down along the trees at a stiff canter.

Blake and his foreman stopped at the corral and sat several moments, talking. Then abruptly Clyde wheeled his horse out, ran across the barn lot, and into the bottom of the trail Jeff and Laur had climbed out of the valley. Some minutes later they listened to the quick drum of his horse as he went past.

"So Bob was right, after all," Laur murmured as the sound of Clyde's animal was fading into the stillness.

"Looks like it," Jeff said, watching her closely.

Alarm all at once brightened the look of her eyes. "Jeff . . . he may be headed back to the mine," she said. "We have to do something. He'll find Bob there. And Bob said he was going to sleep."

"Nothin' to worry about," Jeff drawled. "I know a quicker way to get there." He eyed her intently, asking: "From now on anything goes?"

"Yes, Jeff," she said. "I was a fool to trust Tom. We'll fight this any way we can."

Jeff pinched the end from his cigarette as he said: "Then I'll handle Clyde. You ride over and get the crew started back with the herd. If you don't hear from me before dark, bring 'em right on through and out our lower gate. Then head straight down into the desert for the seep." He gave her a long, steady look, reading something in her tenseness and pallor that made him say gently: "The Tom Blakes of this world have been foolin' people since the beginning, Laur." When her expression didn't change, he added: "And folks like Bob White balance things out. Don't forget that."

His words did bring a change in her now, softened her look and put a warmth in her eyes. He had been worried about her a moment ago. Now, as he turned and left her, the worry was gone.

He climbed on up the slope, keeping wide of the trail, heading for a ridge he knew would take him to the cañon rim above Morgan Blake's mine in much less time than had he followed the twistings of the trail.

Three miles farther on, his horse threw a hind shoe, crossing a bad stretch of rock. In another quarter mile, the animal was going lame and Jeff had more than lost any advantage the short cut had given him.

From a tree came the angry scolding of a squirrel, and Bob White came awake with the instant alertness of a man whose instincts are in tune with his surroundings. He rolled over and looked down across the saddle he had used for a pillow, hands resting at either end of it.

200 yards below lay Morgan Blake's cabin. He had warily rejected its comfortable bunk in favor of climbing this slope and sleeping well away from the place. Beyond the cabin, staked out on a patch of grass alongside the creek, stood Fred Byrne's buckskin horse.

It was the horse, head up, ears cocked attentively and looking this way, that told him the rest of the story. His right hand closed on the handle of the holstered Colt he had pushed in under the saddle fork before going to sleep. The squirrel's chattering stopped abruptly and the stillness ran on, unbroken, except for the faint murmur of the creek.

Something moved off to his left, almost at the limit of his vision. He turned his head to see Clyde Mould, standing less than ten yards obliquely downward from him. The Bellows ramrod was in the act of turning to face him, lifting a carbine to his shoulder. And by the man's look of utter amazement Bob realized they must have simultaneously discovered each other at this exact instant.

He moved with no conscious thought, rolling to clear the weapon and whipping it up.

Clyde hurried his shot, and gravel spurted from the ground a foot from White's face. He took careful aim at the big man's right shoulder and shot him as he was levering another shell into the chamber.

The bullet's impact twisted Clyde halfway around. But instead of dropping the Winchester, he doggedly whipped the breech shut and lined it again. Bob's second bullet caught him fully in the chest and pounded him backward as the carbine cracked once more, pointed upward.

Bob was on his feet before Clyde hit the ground. He ran in on the man and kicked the carbine from his grasp as it was swinging around at him. Clyde lay there, face down, coughing pulpily, a muscle spasm clawing his hands into the gravelly earth. When he could get his breath, he looked up and cursed.

White sat on his heels looking at Clyde until the man's voice choked off. Then he said gently: "Sure, get it off your chest. But you should be namin' Tom Blake all these things."

Clyde was fighting for breath for several seconds, and Bob waited until he lay quiet again before drawling: "Blake sent you up here to be killed. He was through with you."

A blend of uncertainty and anger contorted Clyde's face as he gasped: "That's a damned lie! Tom didn't even know I was comin'."

Just then a sound rode up out of the cañon, and, looking downward, Bob saw Jeff ride out of the trees below the cabin. The look on Clyde's face told him that time was running out and he said brusquely, impatiently: "Take a look down there. It's Jeff. He came across here ahead of you and climbed up where I could see him down along the trail. He waved his hat the minute you showed yourself. So all I had to do was wait here while you walked right in on me.

Blake knew it would happen . . . he fixed it with Jeff. This leaves him in the clear, if you want it like that."

It was a wild chance, a gamble. While he waited, Jeff rode up, and White drawled: "Nice goin', Jeff. He walked straight into it."

The Bellows foreman didn't see Jeff's puzzled look. He was staring hard at Bob. He labored to speak.

"Tell . . . tell the girl that Morg was killed . . . that Tom shot him after. . . ."

Bob waited, tense and expectant, for more. But the words didn't come. A sudden spasm turned Clyde rigid. The man's eyes were pleading with him, so Bob said quickly: "Tom Blake knew Morg had run onto a rich vein? He was trying to get the outfit from Laur?"

Clyde's dying look was one of gratitude. He gave a brief nod, then all at once went limp.

And Jeff, standing beyond him, drawled in an awed way: "There's the pay-off."

VI

Dusk shrouded the shapes of the stunted trees at Cottonwood Seep as Bob rode in on it and swung over to Macklin's caved-in well. The first faint chill was thinning the day's furnace-hot breath as he set to work. And for the first time since he had been picked up there at the desert's edge by Laur and Jeff, he was unsure of himself.

He knew less than nothing about the use of Giant Powder, and now he realized what a chance he had taken in convincing Laur and Jeff to drive the herd out here with a promise that there would be water for the cattle.

He had packed a case of the stuff, a coil of fuse, caps, a crimper, and a shovel on his animal. By the time the last light had given way to star-dusted blackness beyond the peaks to the west, he had buried the case ten feet down in the well and shoveled solidly packed sand on top of it, setting his blast as well as he could, remembering his conversations with Byrne.

Now, as he lit the fuse trailing out from the lip of the hole and took a last look at its glowing end before he climbed into the saddle, he knew that he had done everything he could. He had no notion of how long it would take the fuse to burn down. So, when he had ridden 600 or 700 yards out from the seep, he tied the horses and started gathering dead branches from the clumps of sage and mesquite nearby.

He was squatting there when a thundering blast jolted him sideways. Over the ringing of his ears, he heard the horses nervously shying and chunks of earth falling close by as he picked himself up, looking off toward the seep. He could see nothing, and now walked across to his horse and rode back there.

Gradually, in the starlight, he could make out the vague outline of the hole. He reined in, a slow grin patterning his lean face as his eye picked out the details. The Giant Powder had blasted a hole the shape of a funnel that was a good forty feet across. Standing his horse on the torn rim, he saw a small pool of water reflecting the starlight at the center of the crater. During the two minutes he sat there, the pool grew bigger, rising in the hole.

Twelve miles away, just short of the desert's edge, Laur and Jeff, riding point on the herd, caught the distance-muted pound of the blast, and Jeff dropped back to tell the crew to push on faster.

Far above the desert, Tom Blake stood on the porch of his sprawling house, not much enjoying an after supper cigar. Clyde was long overdue from his ride up Scalplock and the man's absence was suggesting some uncomfortable possibilities. Then one of the crew had brought in strange news an hour ago. Riding the east slope of the foothills, just short of sundown this man had seen Singletree's shipping herd headed south toward the line of Singletree's lower fence. The news had given Blake a jolt, ignorant as he was of the herd having been moved at all from the ground where today's gather had been made.

So he was standing there, mulling over two facts of which he couldn't make head or tail, when his eye caught still a third. Far out toward the obscure horizon of the desert he saw the sudden glow of a cherry-red flash. It was instantly gone, and for a moment he wasn't sure he had seen it.

He was a man intolerant of the things he didn't understand and now a sound that was more a jar than anything audible struck his senses.

A moment later the voice of a crewman drifted across from the bunkhouse, drawling: "Was that blastin'?"

"Who'd be touchin' off Giant Powder this time of night?" queried another voice in mild derision.

But it was blasting came Blake's instant conviction.

He looked out into the darkness shrouding that vast low country once again, carefully remembering the precise location of the flash. He knew each detail of the desert so well that presently he decided the flash could have come from but one place, Cottonwood Seep.

It took a little longer for his curiosity to prod him into remembering Macklin's abandoned well. But once he saw the well as the only thing at the seep to suggest a need for blasting, he shrewdly tied it in with the moving of Singletree's herd. It could be done, he was thinking as he considered the possibility of enlarging the well enough to water that much stock.

This partial understanding of what had been so obscure several minutes ago did little to ease his feelings. He had one more disquieting thought — that Clyde might be dead, that he might have talked before he died. Before his uncertainty became intolerable, he swung around, went into the living room, and crossed it to the gun rack in the back corner.

He was going to ride out there into the desert tonight. If his hunches proved out, he would have a few answers to a lot of questions in his mind. It wasn't in him to wait hours longer, days perhaps, before these strange uncertainties were unraveled.

■ ■ ■ ■

Jeff was somewhere off there in the darkness near the hole, helping the crew work
the herd into water, and Laur and Bob had
had the fire to themselves these past ten
minutes. A vast tiredness held Bob here,
willing now to let others do the work. Looking at Laur, sitting across from him, the red
glow of the coals throwing strong shadows
along her face, he wondered if he would ride
straight on south from Alkali tomorrow
when the herd had been delivered. The
thought prompted an indefinable regret that
he was too tired to analyze.

Laur hadn't said much during the midnight meal. The shock of the recent events
would take a long time to wear off — if it
ever would.

Then, as she caught Bob's glance fully
upon her, a warm smile lengthened the line
of her lips, and she said: "Why couldn't you
have come sooner, Bob?"

Her words didn't demand an answer. Yet
Bob, sensing the closeness that lay between
them now, wanted to say something and was
trying to think what it would be when Jeff
drifted up out of the shadows.

Jeff was walking his horse and the way he

was looking off beyond the fire, back toward the hills, made Bob push erect, asking: "What's wrong?"

"Not sure." Jeff said softly. "Thought I heard something movin' out there."

Bob sauntered away from the fire, trying to hear a sound over the uneven bawling of the cattle. Close to his left loomed the shadow of a mesquite thicket. He was edging toward it, when a high shape materialized out of the shadows.

It was Tom Blake. He let his big red horse come close to the fire before tightening rein. He looked at Jeff, then at Laur, smiling affably.

He said: "So you're the ones!" If he noticed the tight, frozen look that Laur gave him, he showed no sign of it as he went on: "We heard that blasting clear up at the house. I got to thinkin' maybe I ought to know what was going on, that maybe Clyde was mixed up in this some way. So I came on out."

Bob left the thicket and came back to the fire as the silence dragged out.

Blake saw him, shifted slightly in the saddle to face him before asking: "Isn't someone going to invite me to get down and have a cup of that coffee?"

"Sure," Jeff drawled, "help yourself."

It wasn't much of an invitation and Laur's silence was quite noticeable. Yet Blake swung stiffly out of the saddle, dropped reins, and came over to the fire, rubbing his hands, saying: "Winter's in the air tonight."

Bob's glance went over Blake carefully until he was sure that the man wasn't carrying a gun. Then he looked at Jeff, seeing the cold, angry way the Singletree ramrod was eyeing Blake.

He thought — *Jeff'd have it out with him now.* — a moment before Jeff softly said: "Tom, Clyde's dead."

Blake's look showed a strong surprise. He had been about to reach down for one of the tin cups at the edge of the fire. Now he straightened, hooked thumbs in the belt of his trousers, and looked across at Jeff, asking: "How did it happen?"

"He talked before he cashed in," Jeff's voice intoned, ignoring the question.

Over a three-second interval Blake said: "I don't understand, Jeff. What did he say? Who killed him?"

"I did," Bob put in.

Blake's glance whipped around at him, showing a rising anger. "I suppose you had good reason?"

"Good enough. He was shootin' at me."

For a moment Blake stood there, thinking out what he was going to say. He looked down at Laur, asking: "Does this have anything to do with what we were speaking of this noon?"

"It does." It was Jeff, not Laur, who answered him.

"Jeff, you'll keep out of this," Blake said imperiously. "I've been having trouble with Clyde, as you know. I insist on knowing everything you do about him." Once more he looked down at Laur. "Go ahead. What did you find out?"

Her reply was unexpected, an almost vicious outpouring of words: "You killed Dad and now you have the gall to show up here, still trying to . . . to. . . ."

As her voice trailed off helplessly, Tom Blake stiffened, steadied visibly.

It was almost, Bob thought, as if having this out were in some way a relief to the man.

Tom Blake said scoffingly: "Laur, what nonsense you're talking! Clyde said that . . . and you believe it?"

She had no answer for him. Neither did Jeff.

Bob drawled blandly: "We found a boot print up in the mine, at the spot where Morgan was buried. This noon when Jeff and

Laur rode to your place, Jeff happened to wonder what kind of a track your boot made. It was the same one we found there in the mine."

At the last split second, Bob noticed Blake's right hand moving. A premonition struck through him. His hand stabbed to his thigh and he had time to think — *Too late.* — as Blake's hideaway arched out at him. His hand seemed leaden, although he knew he had never moved faster.

Blake was slightly stooped as his gun came into line and exploded. A hammer blow at Bob's left shoulder pounded him around. A trained trick of concentration made him use the twist of his body to complete the up-swing of his Colt and without thought he thumbed a shot. He saw his bullet jolt Blake erect before a sudden fading of his vision clouded everything. His thumb seemed not strong enough to draw the .44's hammer back again. He heard Laur cry out. Then he concentrated all his attention on the weapon, seeing Blake as nothing but a blur behind the darkening curtain settling all about him.

He felt the gun's hammer *click*. He squeezed the trigger. The big Colt spun from his feeble grasp and he sensed that his knees had given way, that he was falling.

Beyond that his senses were engulfed in nothingness.

Bob opened his eyes and was first aware of the sky's soothing gray light overhead, of the utter peace of being able to lie there, watching the fading wink of the last few stars. Then the rustling of a cottonwood's dry leaves against the breeze took his attention and he turned his head. He saw Laur, sitting there beside him. Beyond her a fire burned rosily against the dawn.

Now the pain in his shoulder stabbed him annoyingly as he studied her, seeing the warmth in her eyes as she looked down at him. He smiled and tried to say something. But he heard his voice as nothing but a whisper.

"Blake?" he managed to ask.

A shadow crossed her face. "Gone," she murmured. Then an expression he had never seen before touched her brown eyes. It was a look of tenderness, of an awareness of him that was subtly exciting, that gave a hint of some deep emotion within her he sensed was for him alone. And she said: "Jeff should be back with the doctor in another hour. They've taken the herd on." A shyness was in her as she added: "I . . . we owe you so much, Bob."

"Forget that," he heard himself saying quite clearly, surprisingly so. Finding he had the strength to speak, he wondered if he could move.

He lifted his good arm and reached up with it, touching her hair, her cheek.

She didn't draw away.

ABOUT THE AUTHOR

Peter Dawson is the *nom de plume* used by Jonathan Hurff Glidden. He was born in Kewanee, Illinois, and was graduated from the University of Illinois with a degree in English literature. In his career as a Western writer he published sixteen Western novels and wrote over 120 Western short novels and short stories for the magazine market. From the beginning he was a dedicated craftsman who revised and polished his fiction until it shone as a fine gem. His Peter Dawson novels are noted for their adept plotting, interesting and well-developed characters, their authentically researched historical backgrounds, and his stylistic flair. During the Second World War, Glidden served with the U.S. Strategic and Tactical Air Force in the United Kingdom. Later in 1950 he served for a time as Assistant to Chief of Station in Germany. After the war, his novels were frequently serialized in *The*

Saturday Evening Post. Peter Dawson titles such as *Royal Gorge* and *Ruler of the Range* are generally conceded to be among his best titles, although he was an extremely consistent writer, and virtually all his fiction has retained its classic stature among readers of all generations. One of Jon Glidden's finest techniques was his ability, after the fashion of Dickens and Tolstoy, to tell his stories via a series of dramatic vignettes which focus on a wide assortment of different characters, all tending to develop their own lives, situations, and predicaments, while at the same time propelling the general plot of the story toward a suspenseful conclusion. He was no less gifted as a master of the short novel and short story. *Dark Riders of Doom* (Five Star Westerns, 1996) was the first collection of his Western short novels and stories to be published.

The employees of Thorndike Press hope you have enjoyed this Large Print book. All our Thorndike, Wheeler, and Kennebec Large Print titles are designed for easy reading, and all our books are made to last. Other Thorndike Press Large Print books are available at your library, through selected bookstores, or directly from us.

For information about titles, please call:
 (800) 223-1244

or visit our Web site at:
 http://gale.cengage.com/thorndike

To share your comments, please write:
 Publisher
 Thorndike Press
 10 Water St., Suite 310
 Waterville, ME 04901